An
Outbreak of Peace
Responses to the centenary
of the end of WWI

**edited by
Cherry Potts**

ARACHNE PRESS

First published in UK 2018 by Arachne Press Limited
100 Grierson Road, London SE23 1NX
www.arachnepress.com
© Arachne Press 2018
ISBN:
Print: 978-1-909208-66-7
ePub: 978-1-909208-68-1
Mobi: 978-1-909208-67-4

Printed and bound by TJ International Ltd, Padstow, Cornwall.

An
Outbreak of Peace

Contents

Stories

An Exchange	Lucy Smith	8
November, 1918	Annelise Balsamo	14
The Jump-in	Julie Laing	20
Sown	CB Droege	23
Surplus Women	Rebecca Skipwith	27
The Cormorant	Clare Owen	32
The Ituri Forest	Chantal Heaven	40
The Man Who Left	David Guy	48
The Sylvias	Katy Lee	51
The Summit Gain'd	Nick Rawlinson	55
The Spider Plant by my Bed	Lily Peters	62
Canary Girl	Katy Darby	67

Poems

Peaceful	Anwar Jaber	74
Clearing	Nicholas McGaughey	75
Another Rising	Anne Elizabeth Bevan	76
Left at the Cenotaph	Ness Owen	77
Armistice, 1918, San Francisco	James Toupin	78
Girl Looking Out	Sarah Deckro	80
there are poppies and many other flowers	Rob Walton	82
Coffee Table Diplomacy	Rob Walton	84
Living in the Country During the War	Ellery Akers	85
Poppy Day	Karen Ankers	86
Craiglockhart	Steven Jackson	87

Resurrection: the Sandham Memorial Chapel, Burghclere	Mantz Yorke	88
Sympathy for the Oppressed	Corie Feiner	90
The Grass is Waking in the Ground	Sarah Tait	93
The Catwick Blacksmith (*John Hugill*)	Elinor Brooks	94
Music in the Battlefield	Martin Willitts, Jr	96
War Diary in 1/72 Scale	Peter Kenny	97
Almost Standing Still	Peter Shaver	98
Burdock	Gerald McCarthy	100
I will tell you how it was	Nina Murray	101
The Return	Peter DeVille	102
The Wheat	Peter DeVille	103
Light	Valerie Bence	104
For Jean Jaurès	Norman Franke	106
Retracing his Steps to the Gunpowder Store	Jane Aldous	108
Footnote to Tet	Ken Farrell	109
Talk of War	Nick Westerman	110

Stories

An Exchange
Lucy Smith

They had all stopped at the edge of the ditch. Song Shaoqing was the last to arrive, slipping and scrambling his way up the banked earth to where the men were standing, rain dripping down their necks and spattering their muddy ponchos. The soles of his boots had worn down and as he slithered in towards them he cursed himself for not re-nailing them sooner.

'Careful there, teacher,' came a voice, strong arms grabbing him to a halt. Peering down into the ditch, Song could now see what the men were looking at. A dead soldier stared at them from the bottom of the pit, although stared was the wrong word, there was a vacant hollow where his eyes should have been. Song swallowed, glad now that he hadn't wolfed his lunch on his way across the field.

'We have to get him,' he said. None of the men looked up. He wiped rain off his face with his sleeve. 'Where's Li Tiefan?' Song searched the men's faces for the ganger, hidden by the darkening clouds overhead and by caps pulled down hard.

'Here, teacher.' One of the figures at the opposite edge of the ditch pushed up his cap. Li Tiefan's mouth formed in a reluctant grin.

'We have to get him,' said Song, locking eyes with the ganger. Li shifted his weight from one foot to the other. 'We have to,' he said again.

Li's nose shrivelled at the idea. 'Bad luck, teacher, to touch him.'

There was a rustling of the men, as if the hollow-eyed spell casting them stiff had been broken.

'Can't we just fill in on top of him?' The voice came from down the line.

'No,' said Song. 'He has to be buried in a cemetery.'

'It's a German. Boss won't mind.'

'Would you want him under your field?' said Song, turning to the ganger.

Li spat into the mud. 'Ach, teacher,' he said. 'This land is cursed anyway.'

'A hundred years of bad harvests?'

Li shook his head and gave Song a resigned look. He pointed his pickaxe at four of the men in turn. 'Jiang, Tung, Qiang, Gao. Someone find them a tarpaulin.'

The chosen men turned to the motionless forms next to them as if they couldn't believe it, then slid messily into the ditch, steering away from the body. The others peered over, pleased only to be watching. The silence broke into a noisy commentary.

'He doesn't look too bad.'

'Turn him that way.'

'He'll be rotten underneath.'

Song climbed down with Li. Close up, the German looked more ghost than man, his features sunken and distorted by the elements, his flesh mostly rotted away, a film of papery skin over his cheekbones. He would be unrecognisable now to anyone who had known him, except in a nightmare. His helmet had been knocked back and there were some thin silvery strands of hair still there on his head. An old soldier then. The men covered him with the tarpaulin and started to roll him up. Song looked upwards, willing himself not to remember the dead man's face.

After they had dragged the dead solider out of the ditch, Song left Li Tiefan in charge of digging over the hole and took Jiang and Gao with him to deal with the body. They hauled it back across the field and loaded it onto a handcart, turning the cart down a narrow, heavily rutted track. In the worsening light the cart was difficult to steer, wheeling in potholes and veering off into smashed stumps of trees. By the time they saw the winking lights of the officers' post at the bend of the track they were sweating, despite the freezing rain.

'Wait here,' said Song to the others as they reached the tent. He pushed open the flap and stepped inside. The floor was laid with wooden pallets to keep the mud at bay and a stove burned steadily in the corner. Lieutenant Watts sat writing at a small trestle table, his jacket removed and slung over the back of his chair. In the corner Roberts, the Lieutenant's batman, tended a kettle on the stove.

'Ah, Johnny,' said Watts, greeting Song.

Roberts gave Song a hard look. 'Going out for a piss, sir,' he said.

Watts waved him off. 'Hear that, Johnny? No bloody civilisation here.'

Song pulled a soggy map from his pocket. Watts would want their progress across the battlefield. 'The Mayor wants it back by Spring,' the order had come. In the abandoned villages and farms there was no sign of such a person, but Mayor or no Mayor, they were working their way across it, collecting scrap metal, filling in trenches, ploughing the blackened mud back into something approaching farmland. All the time fighting the dull dread of the dead. They discovered them as flat shapes on mud banks or in shell holes, the strewn clothing the tell-tale sign. At first they had been mystified by the strange misshapen outfits. 'Why would soldiers leave their clothes lying around? Why would a man forget his trousers?' The German was in remarkably good condition, considering.

As they bent over the map, Watts tapped it with his fingers while Song tried to indicate the area they had covered with a pencil. A bit of added thickness to yesterday's line.

Watts puffed out his cheeks, releasing the air slowly. 'It's a slow business, isn't it Johnny?'

'Yes, sir.'

Watts sat, looking contemplatively at the stove, rubbing his leg.

'Hey, Lieutenant!' The batman's shout came from outside the tent. 'There's another two out here.'

'Two what?' said Watts.

'Chinese!'

Watts looked at Song.

'Dead soldier.'

Watts grimaced. 'Is he bad?'

'Yes.'

'English?'

'German.'

'Why the hell didn't you just leave him where he was?' said Roberts, pushing back inside. Song looked at Watts. Did he really have to answer to the batman? Watts for some reason was silent.

'Well, it's…' Song could feel himself flushing. 'It's not good for the agriculture.'

'What do you mean it's not good for agriculture?'

'It's bad luck.' In the fuggy heat of the tent, Song's eyes and nose were beginning to run. He didn't want to stream from his face in front of Watts and Roberts and felt the burn rise in his cheeks.

Roberts rolled his eyes. 'What's that, some Oriental fairy tale?'

'Never mind,' said Watts.

'The last thing I need is a bunch of Chinks bringing me dead Germans for despatch. Who do they think we are, the Cologne sorting office?'

Watts gave the man a look. 'Have a smoke, Roberts,' he said, tossing him a packet of cigarettes from the table, 'and stop being such an arse.' He turned to Song. 'You'll have to take him to the hospital. We can't deal with him here.'

The hospital was another four miles away. As Song stepped out of the tent he sniffed the icy air, sharp in his nostrils, and braced himself. They had perhaps another two hours of manhandling the cart along the ruined track before they could offload their cargo.

In the now heavy rain, the hospital yard was deserted. A fire flickered in a pit on the far side, wafts of heat reaching them in gusts, bearing a strange, sour smell. Jiang and Gao rolled their noses at the idea of approaching it, instead lighting cigarettes and squatting under a wall for shelter, at a non-proprietorial distance from the handcart.

'Bad place, bad stink,' commented Jiang. 'Better find someone quick, teacher.'

Song trod the duckboards to the hospital door. It was quiet inside, a single ward with a curtain partitioning off the end. As he moved along the row of beds, patients looked up and stared. In France there had been a separate hospital for the Chinese. It had Chinese-speaking doctors, green tea and even for a while some singing birds. He'd heard that it had been dismantled. He didn't know what had happened to the birds.

'What is it? Who are you?' An orderly in a white coat stepped out from behind the curtain. Song didn't know what to say about the delivery waiting outside. He didn't want to speak of the dead in front of the sick, not least when they were watching him so closely.

The orderly's face changed as he studied Song, as if he had realised something. 'Wait here,' he said, disappearing back behind the curtain. Song could hear him conferring with somebody, a female voice pitched low, too low to hear. Song looked up at the electric light, the pool of yellow that it cast onto the floor, and at the way it glinted in the water that was dripping off him and accumulating around his feet.

The orderly reappeared, carrying something in front of him. A pair of boots. He looked awkward about them and shoved them at Song without looking him in the eye.

'What are they for?'

The orderly shrugged. 'We have to burn their clothes.'

Song stared at him. The orderly let go of the boots and they tumbled out of Song's arms into the puddle. He stooped to pick them up.

The orderly opened his mouth to say something and then didn't. He rubbed his nose and looked away. 'There's not much we can do about the Spanish influenza,' he said at last. 'And you lot do seem to go down with it fast.'

Song turned the boots over. They were Labour Corps issue, nailed soles, worn down just like his. Inside the left boot was a metal band, recently cut, a number engraved on it. Song could feel the chafing of the band on his own wrist.

'One of yours,' said the orderly. 'Right?'

The boots still had the scent of their owner, human odour mixed with the leather. Song's company had replaced another with repatriation orders. They had marched singing to the railway and from there they had been carried to the sea. This man must have been left behind.

'The burial?'

'It is an infectious disease, you know. There isn't time for all your bells and chanting.'

The dismissal brought the orderly into closer focus. The intricate blood vessels on his cheeks, the fine hair on his upper lip, the crescent of tiny pink pimples on his forehead, Song noticed them all now, the small, ugly and uncompromising differences between the orderly and the man whose boots he now held. He hugged the boots tight to his chest and bowed slightly. It would be an exchange then. The wretched departure of his countryman to be paid for with the grim arrival on the handcart. A rightful exchange, whether the orderly knew it or not.

Outside, the fire smoked and smelled worse. Jiang and Gao had given up on the cigarettes and were gripping themselves close against the whipping rain. Gao was humming a tune, a repetitive buzz to soothe a fretful child. He broke off, his eyes pausing on the boots.

'Alright, teacher?'

'Let's just go,' said Song. As he turned away from the men he felt a miserable fury rise from his stomach and up through his chest and a noise choked out of him, carried off on the foul-smelling, gusting wind.

November, 1918
Annelise Balsamo

There were signs; she looked for them. The way it was no longer possible to see any of the stains on the wall furthest from the bed because it was too dark, the way the noises outside no longer included the cries of merchants, the way her whole body felt, worn so thin she felt transparent against the grubby sheets.

Her shift was almost over.

In the last hours of her shift – when the stains faded and she became increasingly threadbare – the men she saw were almost mute with drink. Most were incapable of anything physical; perhaps a clumsy, stumbling clinch and a missed kiss. Sometimes they went face first into the mattress and she rubbed their backs. They often wept. She sang lullabies to the really distressed ones.

But it wasn't always tender. Being unmanned by drink could equal rage as easily – as quickly – as it could equal grief. Manhood, she had learnt, was a serious business, particularly in front of a semi dressed lady. So for some men, there was no weeping. And from her, there were no cosy lullabies or soothing murmurs. No. In those moments, she was a combatant in a dark battle. It was war. The bed suddenly became a no man's land rather than a land of plenty, and she would move to place it between them. They hurled words at her, and lashed out with half-cocked fists and unsteady feet. But she, not stupefied by drink, kept out of range. Usually. Not always.

Madame, for all the coin rattling around in her pockets, tried to keep the women safe. But she wasn't everywhere. So she had found a huge ex-fishwife with a strong accent from the south, and had her pace the upstairs, pushing doors open that were closed, and using those impossibly strong hands and arms to

14

drag the most enraged soldiers out of bedrooms.

There had been slaps from men who had found themselves inadequate once they had lain down with her. Eva would call out, when the violence began, and the tough old fishwife would charge in and evict the man.

*

When she had first begun work, Eva had wondered if the men would object to the Marseilles fishwife and the door rule. But she learned, early, quickly, they had no sense of shame.

'I've seen the guts of my best friend all tangled in his hands,' one shrugged when she asked him. 'I have no problem with the lads seeing me in the altogether.'

Slaps and open doors were part of every shift. So was the bed as no man's land. All this she had managed. But the unexpected happened too. Once she had not moved quickly enough – or perhaps she had assumed he was drunker than he was – and a huge Australian soldier had got his hands about her throat. Unable to call out, she was left to trust that the fishwife had her eye to all the doors. She did, but not before Eva had felt a dark veil fall across her eyes.

He was pulled off her – it must have taken more than just the fishwife because when Eva was sensible again, the room was full of soldiers in various states of dress – and tossed out of the place.

Eva had been given a brandy and a half hour.

The violence, the rage, and the grief were hard. She dreaded all of it. But they hadn't reached to her soul. What had got as far as her soul were the endless hours of one man after another, sour breath spewed into her face and heavy bones bruising her inside and out. She was at the edge of something, close to a fatal fall.

*

She looks up at the stains on the far wall. It is too dark to see them. Her soldier is asleep on the bed. She feels the energy change in the building – everyone is on the move. It is over for another day.

As the fishwife heaves the dead drunk soldier from the bed,

Eva squats over a bowl of hot water that has been brought into the room. There is blood up and down her thighs, and the water is agony against her private parts. Rubbed raw, she can hardly stand the pain.

*

Getting home is the most dangerous time of the whole day. Eva leaves by the back door and soundlessly slips into the dark alley. The front door is, obviously, impossible; there are hungry men lined up and down the footpath, unbounded by the war and without any pity for either themselves or anyone they encounter. The alley is much safer. The women leave together, dressed shabbily and in as many layers as they can find. Frumpy hats. She has been known to blacken her face with ash from the fireplace so as not to be targeted. Walk quickly and don't meet any eyes. Take the back streets as much as possible. Hide in doorways if there are any footsteps.

But tonight, Eva is alone. And after only a couple of steps, after only a few turns, she knows she will struggle to make it home. Her thighs, she can feel from the slippery stickiness that seems worse with each step, are dark with new blood, and she aches in layers from her breasts, down her ribs, her stomach and groin, hips and bottom. She can still feel the hands that have clutched her over the stretched minutes of this day – thin hands with black fingernails, fleshy, pink hands with almost no fingernails, hands with dried blood, hands missing fingers.

She slips on the stones, it takes her every bit of will to stay upright. The effort of it turns her stomach over and she hiccups and then vomits – only a tiny amount, a teaspoon really. There is not much in there. She leans heavily against a wall. She can feel the cold of the brick through her coat. She wonders if she can find a place here, in a doorway, to sleep the night. She can't go back to the brothel – there are no beds free for a start – and she can't bring herself to breathe in the fug of men looking to celebrate finding themselves still alive by squeezing the life out of women like her.

One man, only today, had stammered as he hung over her: 'This ... alive ... this is alive.'

She had nodded – he was paying after all – but it was bitter. Crushed beneath him, she was struggling to breathe.

Madame – 'it could be their last chance to wreck a bed' – always impressed on the women that these men faced death – Death! (she was dramatic). Their last chance! Eva has seen so many last chances, it's almost a joke.

*

She sits down next to her vomit and the pain in her spine is no longer a dry ache; it feels more like a scald. She's not sure she will be able to get up again. It's not just the exhaustion and the pain. She finds the war has seen her body remade into some kind of terrible topsy-turvy self – legs up over her head, mouth shut and fixed, private parts public, crawling on her hands and knees. The ordinary laws of physical movement seem suspended in her. She might never get up after tonight.

It's cold, she thinks. I need to get up. There is no possible way; without options, she drifts off, letting the cold curl into her burnt spine, numbing the pain in her thighs and groin and hips.

*

'Come and welcome!' Madame likes to cry as the men surge in at opening. 'Or do I mean, welcome and come?' – her follow up, usually as she slaps the woman closest to her. A thigh, a bottom, a breast. Cheers from the men.

*

Eva thinks she might vomit again but there's nothing left in her now.

She hears footsteps but she is incapable of getting up or getting out of the way. It's not like she isn't frightened – her heart is going a mile a minute. If it comes, she hopes it's quick.

The footsteps are unsteady, they weave towards her. They stagger up, stop. She is hardly breathing. Then a heavy settling beside her. Eva risks a look. A soldier, and no doubt he has landed in her vomit.

He doesn't move to touch her so she looks again. He looks young. Wretched. Perhaps there is blood on him; dark patches anyway. There is a bit of a moon but the light is very low.

'I like it here,' he says, his words slurred and muffled. 'It's solid. I don't sink.'

She manages a shrug. It hurts.

'Where have you come from?'

She's not sure about the question.

But he looks at her, as if he is interested.

'That way,' she says, and lifts her hand to point down the alley.

'The fighting, I mean. What fighting?'

'No, not me,' she says. 'I don't fight.'

'Not a soldier then?'

He must be far gone, she thinks, to mistake her for a man.

'No, not a soldier. A woman,' she says softly.

'Oh.'

There is silence. And then:

'They're saying it's over,' he says. 'But our orders are to return to the front tomorrow.'

'I'm sure it's almost over. Maybe they'll cancel the orders.'

'Yes. It's been nice here. Bits of green grass. Food. Drink. Nice ladies.'

She wonders if she has seen him over the last week. She wonders if they have shared a bed.

A movement and a plucking. She recoils but it seems he wants to hold her hand. She surrenders to it.

His hand is cold and utterly without threat.

It's not fair, she thinks, as a wave of tenderness sweeps into her.

They sit for a long time; Eva catnaps. Suddenly, she's jolted awake by a question.

'What will happen tomorrow?' he asks.

'Nothing,' she says. 'Nothing will happen.'

'So tonight we should try to sleep?'

He is fumbling in the dark, and she recognises the undoing of the buttons on his coat even though she can barely see it. Her heart flattens in her chest. But something is different, he is not clambering out of his clothes, but inviting her into the warmth of his greatcoat. He pulls the cloth about them both. The heat of his body reaches out to her. There is nothing taken. Eva falls, willingly, into sleep.

The Jump-in
Julie Laing

Sean's right, I'm the tallest, but Jamie's older looking. He's no' having it, doing Jamie's squeak, acting the big man and saying, *Soon as he opens his mouth he'll get ID'd. Squeak, squeak, the birds have deeper voices than him.* Haha, that's funny, and we're all laughing. Jamie's lost it too, trying to squash the squeak down (not even starting to break) but he knows I'm going in now, so he's part of the laughing too. Then I'm not, cos I know I'm going to be the one, and I'm getting para with all their eyes sideways at me, and I feel myself smirking not smiling. All eyes checking if I'm up for it, then I'm looking at my phone and 21:49 flips to 21:50, slow enough to watch the numbers change. Never seen that before. Mental. C'mon.

It's closing soon, c'mon, someone's saying, then a wee shove from somewhere and I'm checking who's coming up the street for a last minute chance that I don't have to do it. Reprieve. Is that what that means?

What about him? I says out loud and I'm nudging, nudging towards that wee guy heading for Shop-o-late. He'll be up for it, defos, skinny hollow face and nothing to tell you his age. But older than us anyways, so I'm heading over with my legs too slow (he's fast) and he's in and the shop doorbell goes ping then pong behind him in my ears too loud.

Funny seeing us lot at the corner from here like I don't know us. Total jailbait, haha, look at us. Everyone's jumping around in the shadows like a ball of pins, mental, trying to keep it tight till we've got the drink, but mad energy's fizzing everywhere and jumping across to me and crackling up my fingers before I'm even halfway there. Legs getting it together now, then Sanjay handing me the cash and his fingers are sweating – his dad would proper kill him – and Fergie passing the blunt to calm me down. Deep, deep pull on it.

It's happening! Big rush through me, arms cold and stomach shaking, and not wanting to, but the rest of the night's hanging on me. Hollie's hand on my back. Warm and wee, and I want to touch her, but she's turning into a shove. *C'mon you can do this,* then laughing again. Their voices all jangly and their words not getting through the rushing red in my ears. The whitey's coming up from my stomach and if I don't move now now now…

Right, a minute, I'm saying – out loud?

…and I'm jumpjumpjumping it out, and the ground's smacking me back into myself from the feet up and the coins are spilling out my hand onto the pavement, haha, making golden thuds somewhere and someone's fingers are in my palms again rolling my fist round the money saying, *Watch it you that's all we've got.*

On you go, man.

So I move forward. Step, think, a step, I think, step, then knowing, knowing my legs will take me there and arms falling into line too, still holding in my hand the things that must not be lost. Head blood flowing back to feet and fingers making me fit my body again and then ping, I'm in and pong, the door whooshes behind me.

Yellow glare. Fridge hum. Smell of bleach and sweets. Skinny hollow cheek guy bumping past me to the door. A wee shifty round, nothing doing. Don't stop, keep going, or you'll lose it, not too slow, slow down. Fumbling, coins shifting in hand, starting to slip, tighten grip. The hum gets too big for the shop.

Have I been standing still?

He'll be watching. Got to move. Don't look up yet, and hold your shoulders back, straighten up, I'm saying in my head like I'm somebody else on the way up to the counter. Then I'm there, my hand down flat on it for a second then up, straighten up, and while he's watching the damp print shrink away to nothing I look him at him and I know he knows. And his eyes are on me, taking me in, and I'm checking out the bottles behind him like there's a choice or something. He knows fine well and waits. Booming, booming in my ears and my faraway voice is asking for a bottle of blue raspberry MD. Please.

Eighteen, are you? he's saying, looking at me, waiting. Ping… eyelids drop down…pong. He looks to the door.

Aye, I says inside my throat, and he goes between watching whoever that is (don't look round) and getting the bottle. He's asking if I want a bag (5p extra) so I nod cos my mouth's too dry to get another word out. Someone's behind me now, sighing, breathing too cool on my neck and making me shiver. I'm bundling the damp smash into the shopkeeper's hand and a penny sticks to my palm. You can see his skin pulling away, but taking it, and asking if this is the right money. I shrug and he dumps it in the till, all into the one slot. He'll have to sort that later.

He's pushing a blue bag along the counter without looking at me. Sticky fingers pull plastic open with a whispery noise and I'm putting the bottle into it and he's saying, *Yes sir, what can I get you?* to the person who sighs with cold breath behind me. Fingers tingling, breathing high, floor shifting under my feet until I move along the aisle. Relief, relief, relief. Pringles, I'll be having those – what am I doing? – and into the bag they go. Lead's creeping down my thighs making the door an impossible goal.

Ping…air comes back, whoosh, and it's suddenly…pong… dark on the street.

I hold up the booty and it kind of glows green from behind in the light from the shop and the corner whoops. Yaaaas! A big surge bolts through me and the ground feels real again. I'm turning right, left, right towards the park, shoulders straight, tall for my age I am, swinging my arms, and they're running up behind me, laughing, screaming, tripping, falling. A mad following.

Sown
CB Droege

'It'll all be over soon,' the spirit said. It wasn't ominous or threatening. It was almost jovial. As jovial as the spirit of a scythe could be.

'I'm going to die of hunger.' Nadzia said, weakly, then stopped walking, and stood in the silence, knowing that the spirit could not speak to her when the scythe was still. The blade of the forsaken tool lay on the ground behind her, dust-covered and chipped from being dragged from farm to farm across the countryside. She raised her face to the breeze, which refreshed her after walking in the hot August sun for so many miles while the spirit chased her. She took a deep breath, then started again down the road, giving the spirit its voice back.

'That's not what I mean,' it said. Its voice was the sound of the blade dragging along the gravel of the road. 'They're meeting in Minsk right now.'

She turned to look at the spirit as she walked. Its luminous face was the reflection of the sky on the blade as it jagged and bounced. 'That doesn't mean anything for me,' she said. 'They talk and talk, and then they stop talking, and things will be no better for me.'

'The Great War is over,' it said sombrely.

'Ha,' she said without really laughing. 'It's over for them, maybe.' Then she lifted the blade into the air. It was more difficult to carry this way, as it was heavy, and she was weak with hunger, but its voice became limited to the sound of the wind running over the pits and cracks in the metal, a sound much easier to ignore.

Nadzia wondered at the motives of the spirit today. It seemed to be less dour than usual. Yesterday, and every day before, it foretold only doom, and spoke to her only of her death and misery. Today, it almost seemed cheery, like it wanted her to hope. Perhaps it did. Perhaps it would derive some satisfaction from seeing her hope, only to have it dashed.

She set her jaw, and reminded herself how poorly her morning had gone. When she walked up to the farm, one she'd reliably found work at all season, the farmer had looked her up and down – his eyes lingering on her too-thin waist, her knotted and dirty hair – and told her that they did not need her help today.

There was another farm a mile or so ahead that might give her a mid-day meal in exchange for a few hours' labour in their corn fields. She would leave the scythe to rest against the gate, and work rhythmically, mechanically without the blade's voice to nag her. Afterward, they would give her a round of bread, an ear of corn, and a few berries for a meal. If she was lucky, perhaps there would be half of a sausage. She wasn't often lucky.

The nearly-noon sun glinted off the blade, and shone the spirit's face onto the ground at her feet as she walked. Its mouth quirked, as the blade whispered to her insistently, 'The famine will be at an end soon.'

'You are trying to fool me,' she said, and grunted as she lowered the blade back to the ground, so that she would not have to look at the spirit's face. Its voice became loud again.

'In a year you will have plenty again, as you had when you were a child.'

'A year!' she snorted. 'We'll see if I survive the week.'

'You will have a loving husband, and soon after, you will be blessed with happy children, who will grow to be happy men and women in glorious new Latvia!'

'Not even a spirit could see such things,' she said. She wanted to ignore the spirit's words, but she didn't know how. She was too weak. She found herself fantasising, against her will, of the life the rattling blade promised her. 'Independent Latvia will not last the decade,' she insisted, repeating arguments she'd heard fervent young men spouting in the fields, 'The Satversmes Sapulce are just playing at what it would be like to make a government. Any moment soldiers will come from somewhere, and their little games will be over.'

'You are wrong, Nadzia,' the jovial note was back, 'Latvia will flourish!'

'Quit your lies, Demon!' she shouted.

The spirit seemed to go quiet for a bit then, letting its rattling voice lapse into the simple noise it was. She heard wheels coming up behind her on the road, and stopped to look. A small man was driving a small cart behind a small horse. She hoped he hadn't heard her outburst. Embarrassed, she waited by a tree and watched the dust rise up behind the cart as it approached and passed her. The driver nodded to her, expressionless as he rode by. She stole a glance at his cargo, and saw a few under-ripe and undersized melons there. Probably bound for the market in Riga.

As the dust settled, she lifted the scythe up in front of her, resting the end of the tool's handle in the dirt beside the road. The breeze stilled, the sun disappeared behind a cloud, and the spirit had no voice for its false promises, no face to leer at her. Slowly, gingerly, she leaned the thing against the tree, and walked away.

At long last, she was unburdened. She could move without its weight bearing her down. She would be free. She would live.

'Take my scythe wherever you go,' her father's dying words came back to her. 'Without it, you will not survive the coming days!'

She stopped, breath ragged, eyes wet with tears, fists down at her sides, trembling. She turned and ran the few steps back to the tree, and grabbed up the handle of the wretched thing, letting the ruined blade drop back to the road.

'You will die before the season is out!' the spirit rasped at her.

'You will shrivel with hunger and lie dead in the gutter beside this very road!'

'Yes, I know,' she said, wiping the tears from her face, forcing her jagged frown into a flat line. She pulled her free hand through her hair, straightened her tattered blouse and skirt. She wanted to look worth feeding when she arrived at the next farm.

The spirit of the scythe laughed and laughed.

Surplus Women
Rebecca Skipwith

Letters arrived. New times were coming, better times. What times peace would bring!

Still, they fought right up to the end, some of them, and so did I – quietly, I mean, so as not to draw the attention of the foreman. Quietly, ever so quietly we kissed, and I was fighting, because Evelyn, she was already thinking about him. *What if he's… what if he can't…?* I took her out to the lavs in the alley where we smoked, and kissed her just to get her to stop thinking those questions, and I held her round her ribs to keep me there and him out, and hold the 'better times' at bay.

And what was it in the end but the same-old after all? Some of the factories stopped producing armaments straightaway and went back to being tram sheds and railway shops. Ours carried on for a few months, and I worked so hard turning those shell cranks I could've kept the whole army running just by myself. I was up before they knocked at the window in the morning, up and running and hauling my arms back in those overalls, feeling the pinch in my muscles till lunchtime at least. She came in every day like she had to drag herself there. Her noggin wasn't in it. Lord knows where her heart was. Lovely little Evelyn.

So I decided if the old world's just going back to old again, women to their men or their kiddies, I wasn't going to be part of that. Oh, I had a man once, showed me his prick, hard as a brass shell casing he must've thought it was, he looked so proud. I took it, jolly enough, but I itched to get out from under and pull my skirt back down. What a telling off I wanted to give him, to think about taking charge of me like that. To make such a maul of it all. Oh, no. Not for me. So I'm gone, and far away.

The last three days I've got woken not by the knocker-up, but by the ship's bell.

'Morning, darling!' That big girl in the green hat, out on deck again.

I haven't asked her name yet, but I might. A wink and a little look, and then she stands up at the rail, holding on with her lovely fat canary fingers. They've seen some action, those fingers. There's a wind got up and it's blowing her long grey coat about like a flag.

'Looks like we'll get some rain in a bit.'

'I shouldn't wonder.' We're well out to sea now. Haven't seen nothing on either side since teatime yesterday.

'You got a letter where you going?' she asks me.

I have got a letter. A little house, just big enough and quiet enough, and a bit of work on a farm. Never even touched a sheep in my life, but I can turn my hand to most things, and I never lost all that muscle. I've got another letter too, much more precious, much less tidy and polite. I've got both letters, but I'm not sure enough about her to say about either of them.

'Girl I'm sharing with has got a husband lined up. Never met him of course. Probably a halfwit or a strangler. Acting like he's some foreign prince,' she eyes me. 'You got one lined up?'

'I'm not much for a husband.'

'Me neither.' She's got a cigarette out of the pocket of her overcoat. 'Had one once, that was enough.' She has a job getting a match going in the wind that's coming off the sea, but she does it eventually, sucks on the cigarette and then points it at my left cheek. 'How'd you get that?'

'Same way every other body did. Sparks off the trucks. Shell went off.'

'Crying shame.'

I shrug because I hardly feel like that. There's a hundred women in this boat with a scar, or something missing. Holding their suitcases in yellow hands at the ramp at Plymouth. I read

28

in the *Echo* they called us 'Surplus'. Me, I'm calling it a blessed hope. Praise be. I'm moving on to happier things.

'Who you sharing with anyway? I've not seen you about with another girl.'

I shrug again, send her a sly wink, a little pat on the letter in my pocket, and watch her smile around the cig. Can see her thinking things.

*

When the accident happened the men had already started following their own letters home. There were good surprises and bad for the girls who'd been waiting. I couldn't hardly look at Evelyn in those days, even though I felt sick for wanting to. She moved around the machines like someone who was having a dream of a completely different place, and just then I thought I knew exactly what that place was.

The new-old better-worse times were here at last. Some of the women had left the factory already and men taken their places. The women's bunkhouse had emptied and I used to see some who lived on the same terrace as me in their kitchen windows of a morning. The men who used to shout at me in the road by the factory on account of our wages had shut up now the other men who had something real to shout about were home, though most of those ones were as quiet as an empty shoe.

We were fitting on the fuses, me and three others, and Evelyn over the way at shelf 31, taking the trolley back and forth. It was quieter in this block, away from the lathes. We had some chat about the girls' fellas, and Florrie Needham that was going to join the new women's labour movement. I only had half an ear for them, listening for when the trolley would roll closer. I felt it all across my back and up my neck each time she got near, a prickling sort of thing like something would happen, like the nearness of her was almost as good as her pressed up against me. She had a thin little body and was all smothered up in those overalls, but we might have been undressed and standing tight

29

together for the way my skin felt her. Here she came, the hollow scrape and clatter of the trolley wheels making a huge metal sound off the brick walls. Then it just seemed to stop.

There wasn't any big bang or flash, just a great push of heat at my side, and no noise at all and we fell over, all four of us. I must have been out for a bit because I just remember Florrie leaning over me and a smell in the air of everything burning.

No one was killed in the whole block which was a great mercy. If we'd been at full production still it would have been a different story. Burns it was, bad ones in some cases, and broken legs. A piece of shrapnel had to be got out of my cheek, and my Evelyn lost her right arm down below the elbow. That was how we both left the factory, and I thought never to see her again. But that was before the better times finally came for me too. Before Evelyn learnt how to be left-handed.

*

The big girl in the green hat – still don't know her name – leaves me in peace. It feels better than I can say to be out in the air. Halfway from that factory, where I had to cling and hold my breath and graft, and halfway to the little place in Clutha where everything will come easy to hand.

These are the silly thoughts I have. I am a silly girl again, white-skinned and giddy. I want to take out my letter, the precious one, look at its heaven-sent words and its clumsy handwriting, but I'm scared the wind would grab it from me. I won't part with it, for all I know the words off by heart. I stroke the pocket where it sits and even through thick wool I can read it with the tips of my fingers.

'… how you cried and cried over my poor arm. I couldn't say anything to you though I wish I could have. I was like an animal with my brain all shrunk down and everything on fire inside and out. But after it all I was so glad because now I had something to show him how changed I was. I knew he'd understand that, even as he understands nothing else.'

I remember how it was opening it, shaking like a factory girl getting news of her fella when it could go one way or the other. How happy I felt after, and tired to death because I'd been in a fight and won it, though nobody thought I would.

Later, after tea in the ship's bare dining room, I creep back to the bunk. I would have been here either way – surplus by nature, you might say – but how much warmer it is to be needed. There she is, the girl I'm sharing with, stuck in her bed and sick since we got out of the channel. I feel my heart so soft towards her, she's been that ill. I crouch right down and take hold of her precious left hand, and she smiles at me all water-eyed and thin, because she knows the sickness and the hard work has been worth it. She sees those better times coming too.

The Cormorant
Clare Owen

The blow struck Kerra right in the middle of her chest, like the hard thump of a cricket ball. Then came the ache of missed breath and burn of bruised flesh followed by the shock, not from the impact itself but the recognition that the fist really meant to hurt her. And it did.

Her mother stood with feet apart and lips pressed shut, eyes dark little lumps of coal that blazed white when she inhaled and raised her hand again.

'You're good for nothin'!' she hissed. 'Nothin'. You hear me?'

'I'm sorry Mammik.'

'Can't even cook a fish?'

'It's only a little blackened…' said Kerra.

'Never learnin' nothin' from me. Always runnin' around the woods with 'im, doin' I don't know what. All your stories. Gone for hours. The good it did you. The good it did 'im!'

'I'll cook you something else.'

Kerra felt the blast somewhere north of her jawbone, a squeal deep inside her ear and then thick silence. She stumbled backwards. Everything had slowed down, even the throb when it came was measured, heavy with effort like the tolling of a church bell. She groped for something to hold onto.

Mother, wiping tears now on the sleeve of her dress, shook her head and lurched from the room.

Kerra waited. But it was over.

She got up and moved towards the table in a daze, stared at the heavy pan and then picked up the two mackerel by their tails. They were stiff and sooty.

It wouldn't have bothered Gawen.

'Them fish'll come in useful,' he would have said if he were here. 'If you don't want them yourself you might need 'em to bribe a spriggan or the robber who's been hidin' out up at Tregglin's cross or to stick under King Casworen's mattress and stink out the royal bedroom. Revenge for the time he put slugs in Queen Meliora's shoes!'

She nodded slowly and carefully laid the fishes onto a hunk of soft bread, tucked them up in a cloth and placed them in her bag. She took her jacket off the peg, pushed her feet into her boots and bent over to lace them up, holding onto the chair leg when the dizziness took her. Then she walked to the door, lifted the latch and let herself out.

She went across the field down to the cliff path. The way to the right looked muddy after all the rain, proper thick clods of mud, so she turned left and kept going until she reached the stile at the top of Klegrow woods. They'd come here all the time three summers back, before Father had his stroke, telling each other tales of lost treasure, battles, family feuds; taking turns to narrate the adventures of a fisherman from Mevagissey who drank too much cider and tried to swim to Jersey, or the imaginary twins, Sennan and Denzil Penprase, abandoned up at the clay pits.

His stories were always better than hers but he'd pick up an idea, like an acorn from the path, and hand it to her, to see what she'd make of it. And they'd walk and walk, following the soft imprints of horseshoes down to the creek, where the stream snaked its way through mud and marsh and out towards the estuary.

There was no sign of any horses now.

And in the middle of the track saplings were growing up through the wild garlic, and dead branches, silver grey, were tangled up with ivy.

She clambered over the roots and onto the trunk of an oak tree that had fallen out across the water. To keep herself steady she turned sideways on and saw the low stone building by the bank. In their tales it had been a gingerbread cottage, a

Dickensian slum, St. Michaels Mount and the tavern up on the moor. It was also a boathouse. As she edged her way further out, a crumbling slipway came into view and beyond that the stream met the wide, flat river. She eased herself down onto her bottom, shut her eyes and tilted her sore ear towards the sun. Then shunting along a bit, she was able to edge her hip, ribs and shoulder down and press her tender flesh against a clump of damp, springy moss.

'Gawen,' she whispered, 'Gawen.'

*

The tide was low and beyond the boathouse she could see a ridge of sand, glistening in the sun. And a large black cormorant. She watched it untuck its neck and raise itself up through an 'S' bend to form one almost straight line from beak to glossy black tail. Then, with a little shudder, its wings unfolded and started to pulse: huge black wings with three layers of feathers, the bottom ones spreading out like a fan. It raised itself vertically before flattening out and beating its way across the river. One long black wing angled down to the water, where, with every stroke, it seemed to brush its grainy reflection in the water.

She sat up.

There was another cormorant standing on a bit of driftwood. Its neck was sleek with a sheen of metallic purple or green, depending which way it twisted its head. Its eye was definitely green though, a shiny emerald bead.

The name meant 'raven of the sea', she remembered that, and that three flying together was supposed to signify good luck.

But there were only two and they seemed unaware of each other.

The first had landed on the far riverbank and hung out its wings like two coats on hangers, the second hopped off the driftwood and tottered towards her.

Gawen had drawn lots of cormorants. In his sketchbook, there were pages and pages of them, a few in pencil but mainly charcoal. Some were just simple two or three lines capturing the bird in flight, the soft curves of its breast and neck, but others were more detailed. And back at home they'd found the passage in Paradise Lost, when Satan sat on the tree of life, 'like a cormorant', 'devising death, to them that lived'. Mother had hated it when they read together. She said they were always locking her out with their fancy games and their fancy words.

When it was only a few feet away, a tremor shuddered up the cormorant's neck. It tucked its head back, yawned and out came a belching sort of squawk. It was such an odd and unexpected sound that Kerra laughed.

It turned its head in a series of little jerks and glared at her.

'I'm sorry,' she whispered.

She'd never been inside the boathouse but it wasn't locked and although the hinges were rusty, she was easily able to drag back the big doors at the top of the slip. It seemed dry inside, that was something, but the ceiling was low and the three small windows let in very little light. At the far end was an old stove on which sat a chipped mug, an iron kettle and two rusty tins. Kerra twisted off the lids. The first contained some hooks, a ball of string and a gutting knife and the second was filled with biscuits, hard enough to break your teeth. Two deck chairs were propped up against the wall by a narrow metal camp bed with an old sagging mattress turned on its side. That was it, apart from a rowing boat and set of oars, the varnish long since blistered and flaked away.

She could make a fire, there was plenty of kindling lying about, and a bed was more than she'd hoped for.

It was hard to know how long she slept but when she woke the cormorant was still there, sitting on the bank and giving her the eye. She reached into her bag and pulled out her lunch, tearing off a bit of the crust and throwing it towards the bird, but it didn't come any closer. She threw another piece into the grass. The bird turned its head and looked upriver but she knew it was biding its time, like Gawen used to do when Mother made saffron cake and deliberately left a trail of currants on the dresser. When it got up close to the crust though, it dipped its head, pecked and nudged the bread with its beak and pushed it along the ground. It wasn't that interested after all.

Kerra looked at the burnt fish, the scorched, slashed skin peeling back at the edges, the pale flesh underneath. She picked one up, slid her fingers into the gash that ran the full length of its belly and ripped it open. She was lifting the fan of its tail, about to peel back the bones when suddenly the cormorant began pumping its wings and straining its neck and it jerked open its beak, two wishbones fused around a gaping black hole.

She threw the fish down, rolled onto her side and was sick.

When she'd finished retching and wiped her mouth on her skirt she turned round to see that the bird had jumped onto the slimy stones at the bottom of the slip. It took a step towards the mackerel and delicately, as if using chopsticks, picked up the whole fish in its beak. It flicked its head back and after a series of twists and shudders, it swallowed it whole.

Kerra grabbed the rest of her meal and stuffed it in her pocket. She'd need the bread at the very least as she wasn't planning to go home anytime soon.

Later she walked up towards the road looking for some early blackberries but the only fruit she saw was as green as the stalks.

She found the tree where Gawen used to leave her little props and pointers, a letter to Sennan from her secret lover or the message from a corked bottle found off the coast of Sark. He never owned up to them, of course, but she knew his writing, even when he wrote as small as he could and curled the tails of his 'g's into little tiny knots.

She peered into the dank cleft but there was nothing there and she pressed her head against the trunk and wept.

Mother had said that was the hardest thing: being told nothing, nothing in all the months he'd been away. And then one thin letter, dated a year back, describing the boat trip over and the cormorants they saw off the coast of France. His writing, criss-crossing the page like tartan, weaving together snippets to entertain them: William Tremarrak puking all the way and one of the lads from Newlyn telling them how the Chinese tamed cormorants to catch their fish.

And Gawen sent Mammik his love, of course, but the letter was addressed to Kerra. Because Mammik couldn't read. Not that it mattered when the telegram arrived.

And so, as night spread its cloak over the ancient land of Kernow, the fugitive relinquished her fourposter bed for a hideout in the forest. After her battle with the witch, she was wounded and weary and needed no sleeping draught to lure her away from her woes. She was hungry too but she would not starve, for as we know, she was brave and resourceful. She had a plan and after waking with the dawn and splashing the cool river water on her face, she decided to enlist the help of the most skilled fisherman in these parts: the cormorant. But he wouldn't share his skills willingly. Lady Kerra would need to outwit the bird.

She divided a fish into four, placed one piece on a raised chunk of granite down near the water and waited while the sun came up over the trees on the other side of the river. She couldn't throw off the chill of the night so wrapping her arms around her body she rocked gently back and forward to keep warm. She sang too, with such longing that all the woodland birds joined in and before long, the cormorant's head poked up through the long grass. He disappeared almost immediately but popped up a few minutes later opposite the boathouse and launched himself across the mud and onto the slip, whereupon he took three tentative steps towards his prize. Lady Kerra tipped herself forward into a crouching position and slid slowly towards the water but the bird suddenly dived forward, grabbed the fish and flew off squawking into the woods. She didn't see it again for several hours.

In the early afternoon, Lady Kerra of Cornwall put out the

second piece of mackerel, but this time she left it just outside the boathouse doors and waited in the shadow, only a foot or so away from the bait. The bird marched boldly up the slope but stopped when it saw her. She was playing the long game now though, and let him take the fish without a challenge. Sometimes you had to lose a battle to win the war.

The following morning, after a breakfast of hard biscuits, Lady Kerra's resolve was even harder. She sat on the wide doorstep and spread out her skirt like a picnic rug. She placed the third fillet of fish on the hem of her gown and waited. As the bird came up the slip and thrust its head forward to grab it, she was able to reach out and stroke its neck. It cowered a little, moved back, but then jerked its head forward again and she touched its breast with her fingers.

Lady Kerra took the string from the boathouse and when the cormorant next came looking to feed out of her hand she was able to loop a noose over its head and tie it to make a snare. It had to be tight enough to restrict but not panic or strangle the bird. She caressed, soothed and coaxed the cormorant onto the prow of the rowing boat and they drifted downriver with the tide. Just beyond the last of the golden sandbanks it jumped into the water. Lady Kerra leant out over the side of the boat, giving the bird as much line as it needed. It dived down, once, twice and the third time it broke through the surface of the gleaming water, it had a fish.

It tried to swallow, twitching its neck in little spasms, choking and trying again but the snare prevented it. Lady Kerra gently tugged the bird towards the boat, reached into its mouth and pulled out the catch.

It was a bass. A magnificent bass.

At least that's what she would have told her brother. And she'd have told him that she'd cooked it too on a huge bonfire and eaten it all by herself. But there was no fish, was there? And stories couldn't feed you.

Kerra started the long trudge back. Mammik would be beside herself with remorse and terrified her other baben had been taken too.

Gawen would have kept it up all the way along the coast path. There would have been dozens of setbacks and sub-plots before the grand triumph: the huge bass writhing in the beak of the bird. He'd have thought about the fish too, all the adventures it might have had before its inexorable meeting with death. And he'd have given his sister a victory march. Made her carry the bass home, parading it aloft, a peace offering for their mother.

He liked a happy ending. A neat full circle. And it wouldn't have mattered that Kerra was hungry, nor that Mammik deserved to find her own bloody fish.

The Ituri Forest
Chantal Heaven

Paris – July 2018.

'The okapi – also known as the forest giraffe because of its long neck and its elongated tongue – is native to the Ituri Forest of the Democratic Republic of the Congo,' the zoo keeper explained cheerfully.

A flutter of shutters as the tourists photographed the ten-day-old okapi calf. Bijoux pressed her cheeks against the railings, hypnotised by the calf's intense brown eyes.

'Come along, Bijoux. Let the other children see,' Aristide said sternly.

'Did you ever see an okapi in the forest, Daddy?' Bijoux asked the big man with the bear-sized hands.

Aristide's jaw locked.

'Yes.'

'And Congo peacocks?'

He nodded.

'Have you ever seen any mountain gorillas?'

Aristide's nostrils flared as his mind re-visited the traders with their racks of bush meat. He grabbed Bijoux's hand and led her away from the okapi enclosure towards the ice-cream kiosk.

Marjani appeared clutching three ice-cream cones.

'Quick – take them before I drop them! There was only vanilla. The chocolate was sold out.'

Bijoux tucked into her ice-cream not caring what flavour it was. Aristide rolled his tongue over the dome of white confection, deep in thought.

'What's the matter?' Marjani asked.

'Nothing. Bijoux was asking me about the forest,' Aristide replied, his lips relaxing into an adoring smile.

Marjani nodded and led them to a bench beneath a cedar tree to eat their ice-creams in the shade. Aristide had no appetite. Would he ever be able to explain to Bijoux the truth of the Ituri Forest?

*

Bunia – May 2005.

Aristide buttoned up his trousers. He reached up and pulled the toilet chain. He could smell maboke fish being cooked in marantacee leaves – his favourite dish. His stomach rumbled, impatient for lunch.

He climbed up onto the toilet seat and peered out through the slit-window towards the school kitchens. Cook's face was not visible for some reason. He glanced up the road. It was deserted. There were no cars, bicycles or pedestrians. Something was wrong.

He slipped his right hand into his trouser pocket. A clutch of metal bullets jangled in his palm, souvenirs from the last war. He had six bullets in total: one Russian, one American, one Chinese, one South African, one Greek and one of unknown origin. He didn't have any bullets from the current round of fighting for the simple reason that he had spent the last eighteen months in the company of the good sisters of the Convent of Mercy.

The school bell rang. Aristide glanced across at the clump of banana trees in the schoolyard. During break the girls would sit in the shade of the trees and braid their hair while watching the boys play football with an old tennis ball, its black rubber inner-sleeve all that remained of the stamp of approval from Paris bearing the 'Roland Garros' logo.

Aristide studied the ground at the base of the banana trees. There was no shade and therefore it must be too early for break, and yet someone was ringing the bell furiously.

Rapidly he considered his options. The soldiers would stick to the classrooms to begin with. Killing was their priority but after the killing they would go looking for those in hiding. They would be sure to check the toilet block. He had to find a better place to hide.

The bell grew frantic. Aristide blanked out the sound. How about the old latrine? It had not been emptied since the new toilet block went up in March. No-one in their right mind would jump into that pit of fermenting faeces. It was his best option.

The bell reached fever-pitch. Sister Gloria must be ringing the bell, no-one else had the will-power to ring the bell for so long. Sister Gloria was warning him not to return to class.

Aristide slipped his hand into his pocket for reassurance. He selected two bullets – one American, one Russian – and tucked them between his fingers to create a makeshift knuckle-duster. A fistful of bullets in the eye wouldn't save his life but it was better to die fighting than to wait meekly for the machete to strike.

He quietly jumped down off the toilet seat and crossed the concrete floor barefoot. He pushed the door slowly ajar with his knee. An arrow of sunlight pierced his eyes. He raised a hand to his brow and surveyed the schoolyard, his pupils hard and fixed.

The latrine lay behind a row of old oil drums converted into refuse bins. It was a fifty-metre sprint in the open to the latrine. He would be in full view all the time.

He pressed his tongue against the inside of his cheek, deep in thought. It was a habit he had acquired as a terrified child, forced to join the army against his will at the barrel of a gun at the age of eleven. Had he refused to pick up a gun and fight, he would have been slaughtered on the spot. Ever since that time, he had been haunted by the same dilemma: fight on the part of the hated militia or take the opportunity of the confusion to run away and risk becoming one of those hunted down for desertion.

Aristide freed his tongue. He had had enough of being hunted. He sprinted across the yard, his knuckles hard and tight, his legs extended like an antelope in full flight. He reached the oil drums and skidded to a halt behind them. Then he caught his breath and listened. The bell was still ringing vigorously but he could not hear any footsteps. He was safe for the time-being.

The relief was momentary. Now he had to get into the latrine pit. He screwed up his eyes and lowered himself into the swirling pool of warm faeces. His soles touched the slippery concrete bottom. He reluctantly opened his eyes. Filth covered him up to his armpits. He clamped a hand over his nostrils, fighting the urge to vomit. Then he bent his knees and proceeded to spread the foul mess all over his body.

Struggling to breathe, Aristide tilted his head back and gulped in the fetid air. Stinking faeces soon coated his hair, forehead, cheeks and earlobes. He stopped short of his eye-lids. Then he took a deep breath and concentrated on becoming the latrine. The balls of his feet adhered like suckers to the concrete floor. The backs of his legs stiffened like tent poles and became the sides of the latrine. Finally, his shoulders and neck merged with the top layer of swirling detritus.

Eyes open and alert he started to pray. He had done all that was humanly possible to survive. The rest was up to God.

Cockroaches scuttled about the edge of the latrine. Their lustrous metallic wings reminded him of Formula One racing cars. Sister Gloria had shown the class photographs of the Monte Carlo Grand Prix. She had talked enthusiastically about Monte Carlo in a way that had opened everyone's minds and imaginations to the possibilities of the big wide world outside Orientale Province. Sister Gloria had promised to take them all to Monte Carlo if she ever had the money. Everyone had believed her, Sister Gloria delivered on her promises.

Aristide strained his ears and listened for the quick-fire delivery of the soldiers' voices. All he could hear was the bell. Sister Gloria was incredible! She must have been ringing that bell solidly for at least five minutes now. Sister Gloria was a born warrior. Aristide knew that she would do everything in her power to protect Marjani, Jessica, Bijoux, Avril and the other children in her care.

The bell abruptly stopped. Tears flooded Aristide's eyes for the first time in five years. Sister Gloria's angelic wings had finally been clipped. He would not be going to Monte Carlo with her after all.

Now came the screaming. The children must have been screaming all along, but Aristide had chosen not to hear them. He knew from experience that the screaming would not last long. Ten minutes was all it took to silence a school. He wondered how long it took to silence a university. Sister Gloria had encouraged him to study hard to win a scholarship to a university in Paris – so many more people – so wonderfully far away.

Aristide resolved to study even harder from now on. Sister Gloria's death commanded that he finish the work she had set him. His one regret was that he would not be able to study with Marjani as he had planned.

Marjani did not braid her hair like the other girls. Marjani made a collage out of words and framed pictures with her mind. It was hard to believe that Marjani was no longer alive. Aristide frowned, anger briefly taking over the fear.

Male voices ricocheted across the yard. The voices soared, fuelled by the speed of after-kill. Then silence. After a massacre, the soldiers would sit down and smoke. It was exhausting work, killing people.

Muffled voices punctuated the blocks of silence. The soldiers spoke French, the colonial mother tongue. After a while the conversation fractured into two distinct groups: those speaking French and those speaking Hema.

Aristide listened intently, trying to work out how many soldiers there were, how many were only boys, like him, like the children they had just killed. What were their plans now? Which way would they head when they left? He could speak three languages: Hema, Swahili and French. His father was a

Hema; his mother was a Lendu. His parents were dead but they had given him the means of survival: this linguistic ability to adapt and to eavesdrop. Repeatedly he heard the words coltan and cell phone, untranslatable into either language.

He had first heard about coltan from Sister Gloria one Christmas when her brother in Paris had sent her a shiny metallic blue Nokia as a present. They had all gathered around it, fascinated. No-one had seen a cell phone before! The only means of communicating was by the old school telephone that had been put in by the Belgian colonialists decades ago.

Everyone had been fascinated by Sister Gloria's curious cell phone and wanted to know how it worked and what it was made of. According to Sister Gloria, coltan was the new black gold: the vital magic ingredient of all cell phones, and it could be found right here in the Congo – it would make the country's fortune.

Now he knew that white men valued cell phones even more than bush meat. All kinds of people – desperate Congolese people – roamed the Ituri Forest, panning the river beds for coltan and selling it to the highest bidder, and they were prepared to kill for it too.

The shuffling of feet – the recoil of laughter – the rumble of jeeps as the soldiers left. Silence settled on the schoolyard. Aristide crawled slowly out of the latrine. He ripped down the school flag and wiped the filth from his body. It seemed as good a use as any for the nation's patriotic flag. Then he sat down in the shade and prayed for an end to the fighting.

The sun sank below the roof-tops as Aristide entered the school. There were no bodies in the corridors. Where were they? He reached his classroom and gazed with the eyes of a survivor.

Sister Gloria lay across her desk, tiny Avril cradled in her arms. Jessica, Solange, Grace, Mani and Marjani lay in a pile of jumbled joints behind her.

The boys lay in the middle of the room surrounded by their only weapons: books. Bloodied books, trampled books, books of knowledge, books of truth: books of hope. Prince's severed arm was proof of his heroic efforts. Aristide screamed inside, imagining Prince – such an awkward reader – using Sister Gloria's precious books as missiles to defend the younger boys.

Aristide knelt down and delicately slipped his hand underneath Sister Gloria's bloodied hair. Her skin was a delicate pink; too pink for death. He removed the gold cross from about her neck and kissed it.

'Aristide…'

Aristide looked up, startled.

'Marjani!'

Aristide pulled Marjani free from the tangle of bodies and pressed her close.

'Can you walk?'

'I think so,' she said hoarsely. 'But where can we go?'

'To the forest.'

'Is it safe there?'

'Yes,' Aristide answered, with more confidence than he truly felt. He glanced down at the school bell.

'Did Sister Gloria ring the bell?'

'We all did. We took it in turns. Sister Gloria told us not to scream and to ring the bell instead.'

'Did it work?'

'No. Everyone screamed. Even Sister Gloria screamed just before she died. But I didn't. My voice left me. I don't know why. I just fell to the ground and lay still.'

'I understand. It happened to me once.'

'When?'

'Another time.' He looked away. 'Similar to this.'

Marjani nodded. They locked hands and headed for the forest.

*

Paris – July 2018.

Marjani finished her ice-cream and placed one hand on Aristide's

46

forearm. The tips of her fingers stroked his skin. Then she tilted her head upwards. Aristide gulped. There was no escaping Marjani's look. She understood how greatly it disturbed him to see the tourists taking photographs of the okapi and not understanding that those pictures were tarred with blood.

'Thank you, Aristide.'

'For what?'

'Bringing me here.'

'To the zoo?'

'No,' she said, refusing to rise to his deflection. 'Paris.'

'I always promised I'd bring you here if I could. Sister Gloria would have wanted it.'

Marjani nodded.

Aristide twisted his mind away from all the things he had done since they had walked into the forest together, all the coltan he himself had sold, and shuddered. He glanced at the tourists snapping away at the okapi calf with their new cellphones and he wondered if they would buy so many gadgets if they knew the truth of the Ituri Forest. It was impossible to tell. But one thing he did know. He would not be buying Bijoux a cell phone for Christmas, but a paintbox. Perhaps the boy soldiers of the Congo might have liked to paint too.

The Man Who Left
David Guy

There was a man who had lived for a long time on his own. One day, while walking in the woods, he met a woman and they fell into love. One night, a few quick months later, she fell into labour, and while the doctor and his midwives attended to her the man went outside for a walk.

He headed out into the woods and there was met by men recruiting for the army, and very quickly they impressed him into service. He spent many years away, and was forced there to fight incomprehensible battles in unknowable places for increasingly unclear reasons. He became so weary and distraught by this life of constant toil and terror that it was only his dreams of returning to his wife and child that kept him sane.

Eventually there came a battle the army could not win. A bullet struck him in the lung and he fell down among the corpses of his colleagues and stayed there. When the battle drew to a close and the victorious walked among the wounded to deal them their final blows, he lay still and pretended to be dead in the hope that they would pass him by.

The true corpses attracted the crows. But the crows left his body well alone, for his stench was not yet to their liking. The soldiers drew ever closer, and he feared he would soon be found.

'Crow,' he called. 'Please come here and feed upon me, if only for a little while, so that I may look as if I am dead. For if I am found alive I will be killed stone dead, and never will I be able to return to my love, who I was snatched cruelly from, nor see the face of my child, who was born scant hours after my abduction and whom I have never seen at all.'

Even though the offer was a poor one, for if the man was dead the crow would have his whole body to eat rather than a mere moment's bite, it took pity upon him and hopped up onto his face. And as the soldiers approached the crow pecked out his eye.

Convinced the man was dead, they passed on by. When it was safe again to speak, the man thanked the crow. 'And you may have my lung as well,' he said. 'For it is dead now inside me, and shall only rot and fester there around my heart,' and he reached into the bullet hole in his chest and pulled out his lung from within him, much like a magician pulling handkerchiefs from the pockets of his coat.

In thanks for this kind gift, the crow told the man where he was, and how he could get home. The way was long, however, and it took him many years to make his way back. One particularly cold winter in the hills he lost his toes to frostbite, and one especially hot summer by the sea he lost his hand when a mouthful of water stolen from a king's fountain was punished as severely as could be.

It was well into the sixteenth year of his exile when he finally arrived home. He knocked on the door of his old house and a woman answered.

'Is that you?' his old love said.

'It is,' he said.

'What happened to you?'

'I lost a lung to a bullet, and my eye to a crow. I lost my hand for water, and my toes to snow. But all these years I have saved my heart for you.' And he opened up his chest and pulled out his heart and placed it beating in her trembling hands.

'What would I want with this?' she asked. 'What could I want with it? I hardly know you. I hardly ever knew you. You left and the world went on for all of us. You didn't save your heart for me. It was always yours, and yours alone. The dream of me that kept you alive was a dream, and was not me. And it was your dream, and yours alone. Give your dream-wife this heart, and leave me to mine.'

And she handed him back his heart, and went on with her life. And he, eventually, with his.

The Sylvias
Katy Lee

She is about to steal an axe.

Dot is standing in the tool store, drinking in the musty smell of the earth floor. She's in her civilian clothes. She picks the axe up and feels the once loose fitting blouse tighten across her shoulders and upper arm, and she nearly falls over, unaccustomed to wearing a skirt and what she now thinks are wholly impractical heels.

How war changes people.

She takes the axe from the tool store, carries it to her bunkroom and hides it under her clothes in her suitcase. It's her axe, and has been for nearly two years, so she doesn't see why she should leave it behind now that they are finally going home.

Dot had been in the bunkroom she shared with four others, about to pack. She had pulled out her suitcase from under the bed, surprising herself at the ease with which she did so. Throwing it open she immediately saw that her axe, Miss Sylvia, would fit across the diagonal, hidden under the rest of her belongings.

War is over. It ended several months ago. Today, now felling season is over, she and all the other women are leaving Littory Wood, and returning to Bristol, South Wales or wherever they came from.

They are a mixed bunch: factory workers, domestic servants, educated women like Dot, all pitched in together. The swinging of an axe makes no distinction of class. Dot was thankful for the freedom to come and go as she pleased, even if the conditions weren't that great in the bunkhouse, better that, than the over-protective eye of the landlady some of the women had to content with.

Dot knows it was silly to give the axe a name, but she did it anyway shortly after arriving. It didn't particularly deserve a name, but it seemed rude not to. It was just an ordinary standard issue axe, the same given to all the women doing forestry work. But her red cracked hands, with split nails and ground in with grime, now know every mark and defect along its shaft, her hand fits perfectly into the indent on the lower left side.

Very quickly, after a few weeks of being here, each woman had an axe they preferred, one that felt right in the hand. In theory they were all the same, but as soon as they started to swing the axes, the difference could be felt. They all had their favourites.

Dot strokes the calluses at the base of her fingers, and smiles. These are the only medals she will receive for her war effort. And like her brother, she wears hers with pride.

Miss Sylvia, the woman Dot had named her axe after, was never just Sylvia, always *Miss* Sylvia. She was the woman who convinced the authorities that women could do forestry work and do it well. It was Miss Sylvia who got on with proving it while around her others were wondering what the women would wear.

Dot and her team were part of the 'Devon Experiment' four months ahead of the formation of the Women's Forestry Service.

First they worked at Woodman's Well Wood in Lydford, bark peeling for the tanneries and cutting pit props, and then on to Littory Wood, again felling timber for props.

Back in the bunkhouse, stashed away and hidden beneath rarely worn dresses and skirts, a couple of books, her diary and other meagre personal effects, lay the stolen axe.

Beneath it was a bundle of letters from her mother, regaling her with the exploits of her elder brother, accompanied by newspaper cuttings on the progress of the war, as if here in rural Devon such things didn't exist. The letters contained no mention of her younger brother. He had died early on in the war, the reason Dot had volunteered. The grief her mother felt was locked away and never spoken about.

But then Dot didn't mention him either in her answering letters. She too, included newspaper cuttings, and kept copies folded into her diary.

She was particularly proud of one from *The Devon and Exeter Gazette,* just ten days after she and the other women had first arrived at Woodman's Well. The article included two photographs. She was in the top one, second from the left, with her axe resting on her shoulder, smiling. The photograph makes Dot laugh – most of the women in it were still wearing skirts. That didn't last long. They quickly followed the lead of the coal miners' daughters, who had sensibly worn trousers and sturdy boots.

The article received no comment from her mother.

Another cutting, tucked into the pages for February 1918, is equally treasured, although at the time it didn't seem all that relevant to her. The end of the war still seemed like a distant thing and like the rest of the women, Dot didn't really give much thought to what she would do after it. They had talked about it, of course, but most of them were under the age of thirty, and the few that were married, certainly weren't married to men with property, nor had property of their own, so getting the vote had little relevance to them. Dot had kept the clipping all the same.

But now?

Now that Dot is about to return home, now that Dot no longer has a job nor income, now she knows what she is capable of? Now, it does seem relevant. And even more relevant because one of the Pankhurst women is called Sylvia.

She shuts the suitcase with a click. Dot can carry the suitcase comfortably. So long as no one else tries to help her, no one will know it contains an axe with a four and a half pound head.

When she gets home, she decides, she will tie purple and

green ribbons to her axe and prop it up against the doorframe to her room. And there it will remain unused and gathering dust. Getting life back on track, back to normal is the order of the day. But the axe will stand guard, a reminder, a declaration of what Dot and others like her can do, something that, before the war, would have been unthinkable.

Miss Sylvia Calmady-Hamlyn was the first and only travelling inspector appointed by the Board of Agriculture during WWI. She covered the area between London and Land's End. Calmady-Hamlyn was a prominent member of the Women's War Service Committee who reasoned repeatedly and strongly for the inclusion of women within wartime agriculture.
She recruited and placed women workers within forestry, in both processing and planting, and publicised these experiments, such as that at Lydford.

The Summit Gain'd
Nick Rawlinson

The hills are still there.

Ridiculous, really, Henry thinks. There was no reason to have worried. Hills don't just suddenly pick themselves up and move. Not in England, anyway. And certainly not in his father's parish. His father runs a tight ship: hymn books all in a row, not a hassock out of place. He wouldn't let significant geographical features go wandering about without so much as a by-your-leave. It would take an Act of God – or a strongly worded letter from the Archbishop, at the very least – before he'd allow such a thing.

'Thank God,' Henry says. Then he feels a little foolish. There are countries, after all, where the landscape is not so obliging. Where hills don't bat a tuft of rye grass about changing their position. Hadn't his Uncle John told him, once, about a mountain in Egypt that had just disappeared, almost overnight?

John was in the Eastern Desert. He'd served with General Gordon at Khartoum, and somehow ended up working for a mining company, at a place called *Jabal Hamasat* – the Mountain of Whispers. The local Bedouin warned them not to work there. Said, if they had to dig, then they must do it carefully, to caress the mountain, using only hand-picks and chisels. Attack it with machinery and dynamite, and the mountain would take its revenge. Superstitious nonsense, of course, John said, but he admitted the work was hard. Every flake of gold had to be wrestled from rocks that would cut your hand for touching them, in heat that would blister you, even when you stood in the shade.

Then, one night, he was awoken by an almighty roar, like the voice of God himself. Perhaps one of the miners had got frustrated with their slow progress, or maybe some fellow had just been careless, but too much dynamite had been set off at once, and half the mountain cracked, and disappeared. Over three hundred miners, men and boys, were trapped below ground. The survivors grabbed anything they could – shovels, picks, even tin plates. They dug for five days. The dust in the rescue tunnel was so terrible, it was like a living creature, John said: a whirling, burning devil, intent on scratching out their eyes and ripping open their throats. The only way the men could force themselves to go into it was to give their womenfolk pistols, and order them to shoot anyone who turned back. John himself spent so long in that tunnel, bent double and clawing at the rocks like a madman, that when he finally emerged, he couldn't stand up straight. Never did, for the rest of his life.

After five days digging and blasting, the rest of mountain crumbled and caved in. Nothing was left, and no one was saved.

Henry kicks a tuft of grass with his foot. A swarm of little flies emerge, and dance up towards him. The sun catches their wings, and they glow like tiny haloes. High above Henry's head, a skylark begins to sing. Henry looks up, trying to see it, but it is lost in the light.

There's a field to cross before he can reach the hills. It's a closely grazed pasture, full of golden buttercups and cowslips. Henry finds a gate, puts his hand on the topmost bar and climbs over. In the May sunshine, the wood is warm under his hand. It almost feels alive.

The hills are now directly in front of him. Two small, beautiful, rounded chalk hills, side by side. Over the years, they've been known by lots of names: the Barrows, the Berkshire Bubs, and even (according to the locals), Mother Dunch's Buttocks. Henry, though, has always called them Wittenham Clumps.

He sniffs the air. In the hedgerows, the hawthorn is in flower, and stands of cow parsley wave their white lace handkerchiefs in the breeze. Nowhere else quite smells like home.

If he could, Henry would pick up this landscape and wrap it around himself like a cloak. He spent his childhood here, flying kites, chasing friends, waging pretend wars under banners of sticks and goose grass. Whole afternoons making leaf trumpets, or sifting for flint arrowheads in the spoil from rabbit holes, while his father walked nearby, practicing his sermons to the wind.

I will lift up mine eyes to the hills. From whence cometh my help?

Henry bends and finds a small chalk pebble. He rolls it through his fingers. He has a choice. Which to climb first?

Round Hill, on his left, is the bigger of the two. It's shaped like a child's picture of a hill: a large smooth bump with a stand of beech trees on the top, perched like a king's crown. There's an old legend that, if you can trap a cuckoo in those trees, summer will last forever. Henry and his friends had tried. They'd run around, shouting and banging sticks, trying to keep the birds penned in. It had never worked. All they ever did was startle the grazing sheep into lifting their heads for a moment, and staring at them through strange, horizontal eyes.

Henry imagines himself at the top of Round Hill. There's a great view from up there. The river Thames, curving like a shepherd's crook, carrying memories of Oxford as it runs softly towards Henley and London. Sitting on the bank, like a patient, stone fisherman, will be the church of St Peter's, with its famous fourteenth-century bell tower, built as an act of contrition by a local gambler (although he wasn't very repentant: the windows at the top are in the shape of the ace of spades). And on the far side of the river, at the end of a disused Roman road, will be Dorchester Abbey, perfectly at home in its rural surroundings. No over-reaching towers pointing to God here, my goodness no – just a low, square building, as fat and brown and contented as the local cows. There's a tombstone hidden inside the Abbey that Henry loves. It's to Sarah Fletcher, a rather over-dramatic young lady from the eighteenth century, who – although credited with all the virtues tombstones usually ascribe to dead young ladies, such as *beauty, innocence,* the *love and esteem of all who knew her* – still couldn't, it seems, quite cope with the rude jostling of the world, and so died, a martyr to *Excessive Sensibility.*

Henry chuckles. Then he stops.

There was this chap: Henry saw him, on the boat, when they were sailing back to Blighty. He wouldn't go below decks, even when it started to rain. He just stood there, by the railing, clinging on to a lifebelt. Someone put a greatcoat around his shoulders, but it didn't make any difference. His sensibilities had gone. Blasted to shreds.

That decides it. Henry takes the other track, the one that curves to the right, towards Castle Hill.

The sun is hotter now. He can feel it on his back, and he is grateful for the breeze that always blows on a slope. He wishes he'd chosen a different jacket. This one is wool, pre-War and much too heavy for summer. He only wore it because this is a special occasion, and he wanted to look smart.

Castle Hill carries a scar all the way around it, a deep defensive ditch, dug by Iron Age warriors and improved by marauding Danes. It's a challenge for anyone, even without its fierce defenders raining stones and spears down on you. But there is a footpath Henry can follow. It's been cut through the ramparts by generations of feet. Henry skirts a patch of young nettles and begins to climb. It's only a short way, but he feels himself start to puff. For a moment he panics. A memory: of floundering, gasping for air, a poisonous yellow fog. Henry splays out his feet like a skier and shoves himself up the slippery scree to the top of the ditch, forcing his legs to move, left, right, left, without thinking what is ahead of him, left, right, pushing the memory down, left, right. And suddenly, he's through it, and he is standing, panting, on the inner crown of the hill. He's startled a pair of rabbits, and they zigzag away from him, crashing into the brambles that grow beneath the copse that straddles the hilltop.

Henry stops for a minute to get his breath back. Sounds drift up from the valley beneath him, like echoes from another world. There's the jingle of harness, marking the slow, steady progress of Farmer Sheard's horses. And from further off, there's the insistent, nervous growl of a motor car. It must be Doctor Piper, on his way to see old Mrs Hart at the Manor House. Her Pierce was lost in Delville Wood. Now she smokes more than is good for her.

Henry turns towards the copse. He can hear a blackbird, whistling its music hall repertoire. He thinks of going closer. But it will be dark under the trees, and the woodland floor will crackle underfoot with the dry rustle of last year's leaves. They always seem to collect in the dips and hollows. His father claims these bumps were the sign of Iron Age farming, long thin strips for growing vegetables. Uncle John always scoffed at the idea. 'It was a cavalry camp, boy, plain and simple, Roundheads resting their horses before falling on Wallingford in the Civil War.' Henry doesn't know who is right, and it doesn't matter. He decides to stay out in the open. He skirts the wood to the east, and heads for the farthest corner north.

From this side of the hill, he can see the King's Barrow, the final resting place of the last of the Iron Age chieftains, and spread out to the left, the oaks of Wittenham Woods. From somewhere deep within, a skulking fox sends up a brace of pheasants, and they cluck away on whirring wings, like alarmed automatons.

A final few steps, and then he has found what he has come to see.

It's a large beech. Its branches are spread so perfectly they look like the home of a wise, storybook owl. The leaves are newly unfurled, and are a brilliant shade of light green. And carved into the bark, around the whole trunk, there are words.

Many of the trees in this copse are tattooed like this; with the secret initials of lovers, the bold claims of braggarts, and the names of those who, unable to afford a fancy tombstone in the

Abbey, simply hoped to leave some sign of themselves for the ages yet to come. But this tree is different. It carries an entire poem. It was written more than half a century before, and the letters are distorted now, spread and stretched where the tree has grown.

'*As up the hill with labr'ing steps we tread*
Where the twin Clumps their sheltering branches spread...'

Henry knows the poem well enough, but some words are hard to read now. He lets his fingers find their way across the curls and downstrokes, tracing the scars of the missing letters.

'*The summit gain'd at ease reclining lay*
And all around the wide spread scene survey...
Around this hill the ruthless Danes intrenched
And these fair plains with gory slaughter drench'd...'

Henry stops.

He puts his hand in his jacket pocket. His fingers close around the cap badge that he has carried ever since he came back from France. He holds it up towards the tree. In the dappled sunlight, the brass shines like gold.

'See?' he says. 'Old Joe Tubb's poem. It's still here.'

There were times, Over There, when the fields screamed, and the hills vanished. When the trees splintered and threw themselves into the sky. When Henry pressed himself into God's good earth and wondered if he was ever going to get home, or if he was just going to disappear, fall and vanish like Uncle John's mountain. He'd made himself a promise, then – no, not a promise, a prayer. If I get back, I'm going to climb those hills again. Read the poem, once more.

A sudden breeze makes the leaves rustle. It's a low murmur, like pebbles on a beach. The other trees join in, like they have something to say. Henry puts the cap badge back in his pocket. If he walks back to the Vicarage now, he'll be there in time for lunch. His father will be working in his study, polishing the next week's sermon. On his way home, Henry thinks, he'll pick some buttercups and put them in a jam jar. After lunch, he can walk to the churchyard to lay them on Uncle John's grave.

He nods. He's been back for a month, but now, at last, he is home.

The Spider Plant by my Bed
Lily Peters

The spider plant by my bed grows when I don't look at it. Sometimes, I worry it will grow toward me in my sleep. A heat-seeking tendril will claim my nearest ear as its new home. My brain will be riddled with variegated leaves. I will become 'she of the spider-plant-take-over' fame. Then I will fade into memory until those who remember me are lost too.

The spider plant by my bed does not protect me from night visitors. I still occasionally see them around the bed as I drift off. One stands by the window, as if looking onto the street. Another lies on my side of the bed, which, now, of course, is either side. Because I don't share my bed, except with the people who visit at night. One likes to sit on the end, barely creasing the duvet with their featherweight.

The spider plant by my bed is not affected by the weight that presses on my chest as I try to doze. It doesn't concern itself with my need to drift off with the light on. It isn't aware that I am yet to get used to sleeping alone. My tentative smile at the thought of this freedom, when I allow myself to try a grin, is unseen by the plant.

The spider plant by my bed was a gift to myself, from me. I had found myself fearful, once again. Fearful, but not scared. I was on the High Street. A match had just let out. People – real, this time, and loud, so loud and full of the excitement of the day, dressed in striped jerseys – started to press and pool around me. I felt the panic in my chest. I felt the weakness in my knees. I felt a strain on my bladder. I needed to get out of there. I rushed to the car park, sped through busy streets, hit the road.

Then I found myself at the Nursery.

The spider plant by my bed would have been pretty happy to stay amongst its leafy friends. I don't think it wanted to be the first plant in my empty new abode. Nothing cosy about this home, not yet. I think I should have bought a pair. But then, spider plants make new friends in no time.

The spider plant now by my bed came home with me. I'm not sure why I went to the garden centre in the first place. I think I felt safe there. I think, maybe, it made me think of my mum. Odd. I haven't spoken to her for two months. She doesn't know about my residential change. She doesn't know that I know that she was right, those many months ago, when she'd warned me about my choices – specifically my choice of a man who had known warfare.

The spider plant by my bed was bought alongside a bright blue pot and a bag of indoor soil. They threw a bottle of *Baby Bio* in for free. Tear-stained cheeks helped that deal along. Funny, I haven't actually cried for about a week now. As the spider plant is my witness, I haven't even sobbed at the TV programmes that used to make me sad.

The spider plant by my bed is my first pet in this new place. I can't have a real-life animal – the responsibility would be too great. Sometimes I get back from work so late that I don't even bother to turn on the light. The spider plant can't know about the role of the light switch in the arguments of the past.

Why was I home so late? Who had I been with? Angrier now – did I know I had ruined the evening, the day? Was I aware that now it would be impossible for him to sleep?

The spider plant by my bed was never thrown at me from across the room. Its was not the soil trail left on the wall by the window. This spider plant wasn't re-potted with shaky fingers in the middle of a cold March night at the end of a birthday celebration gone wrong.

The spider plant by my bed is sitting precariously on top of a pile of books with interesting-looking, but unbroken, spines.

Sometimes, I picture a scenario in which I have died. In this scenario, my bedroom is a vital piece in the puzzle of my life. I want those spines to tell a flattering story.

The spider plant by my bed is unaware that I still wear his sports socks to keep my feet warm at night. I don't think the spider plant can hear the music I listen to when I want to dance. The spider plant (thank God) can't see me throwing myself around the space that is mine.

The spider plant by my bed is the first of many-to-be. I want to live in a jungle. The chilli plant I bought for our two-year anniversary was killed for the sake of his cat. Apparently, the cat didn't like it. The chilli plant deserved to be left out in the cold. To shrivel, diminish, die.

In return, I killed the orchid. I hated orchids anyway and that was well known.

The spider plant by my bed will witness changes over the next few weeks. It will see framed photos of happy times appear on the newly painted walls. It will learn the shapes of friends' faces. It will be cooed over, re-potted and aided by my green-fingered mother. It may see parts of people it would rather not. It will grow. It will thrive.

The spider plant by my bed sits beside my phone charger. One of its leaves has landed on the cover.

The spider plant knows that I should call mum. The spider plant knows that she could help. The spider plant doesn't understand pride. It doesn't know about the shame I felt and still feel, having put myself in a plant-killing situation in the first place.

I don't want this spider plant – or any other plant or person for that matter – to know.

The spider plant by my bed doesn't know that I haven't told anyone at work, that colleagues still think I am on track for a white wedding and babies. That the handsome soldier they all comment on is gone.

The spider plant by my bed would survive if I visited a friend today. It would cope if it heard my car tootle off to partake in some soul-cleansing, tea-drinking, beach-walking, casual conversation. It would even accept it if I took up an acquaintance's offer of a cinema trip and dinner next Friday night.

The spider plant by my bed wouldn't understand how fearful I am. Not scared – but fearful. The spider plant doesn't know about age and how it matters to people. Spider plants just keep growing and spilling and creating. I can't imagine growing big again. I can't imagine being the size I was before I began to disassemble.

The spider plant by my bed only sees me as the person I am now. The spider plant isn't aware that I once had long hair and a great sense of humour. I should read the spider plant the story of Samson and Delilah.

The spider plant by my bed thinks it is about time I got on with it. And the spider plant is right. This could and should be construed as navel-gazing. The spider plant knows that I should either grow flowers from this shit, or flush the shit away. The spider plant thinks that if I do take up my acquaintance's offer, I should wear the culottes I bought last year but have not yet worn.

The spider plant by my bed knows I should get up now. Its leaves do not understand my Sunday induced lethargy. It always reaches for light, it always soaks in the water, it always photosynthesises. It mends its own broken leaves. It doesn't concern itself with blemishes on its stems. It heals itself from the inside, existing on the basics.

The spider plant by my bed doesn't consider the virtues of procrastination nor the habits of loneliness. It doesn't worry about its place in the world. It isn't expected to be, to do, to achieve certain things. It doesn't put up with, or put out for. It doesn't shut up or shut out. The spider plant is doing existence well.

The spider plant is something to be admired.

I will be more like the spider plant by my bed.

The spider plant by my bed is already working on its first spider buddy. A tiny white and orange flower glows at the end of one of its spikes. In it, I see the future of my spider plant forest. The spider plant wants this forest of freedom as much as I do and is working towards it.

The spider plant by my bed is helping me to start again. The spider plant is ageless, timeless. The spider plant is watered, strong and ready to remain in the world.

The spider plant by my bed seems to rejoice in the weak stream of sunlight that has parted the clouds outside.

The day beckons us both.

Canary Girl
Katy Darby

'Push, Mrs Phillips!'

You bloody push, I'm thinking, flat on me back, staring at the bedroom ceiling and that jagged crack Danny never got round to plastering. I'm exhausted. Queer things pop into your head at these times. Midwife's bent over, staring between me knees like she's inspecting the troops. Suppose she's seen worse; she's trying to be encouraging, anyway.

'Come on Mrs Phillips,' she urges, 'just a few more good goes!'

She sounds like she ought to be on the wireless – voice bright and crisp as an apple, the sort of 'gel' who always *jollies along* and *looks on the bright side*. Had a couple of that type as supervisors at the factory: Miss Evans and Miss Beech. Got pretty sick of both of 'em by the end of the War. Didn't know who we wanted our bombs to drop on most: Fritz or the Misses, as we called 'em. They was the ones responsible for keeping tea breaks to ten minutes, sending us home for the day if we arrived five minutes late, and checking we was keeping up production. And didn't they let us know it!

Here comes another one. Mary Mother of God preserve me, the other girls never said it'd be this bad! Hope you didn't suffer like this, Mary. I expect God went easy on you.

'Good… good… breathe, that's right… nearly there now…'

She's watching progress down there, old Margery. At least someone's 'appy. I put even more effort into the end of the contraction and out of my panting mouth comes a loud moo, just like a bloody cow. I ain't never made a noise like that in me life!

'Was that me?' I gasp. Her hand grips mine – she's got real doctor's hands, this one, cold and smooth as Bakelite – and gives it a squeeze.

'Don't you worry, dear; you make all the noise you need. Anything that helps get Baby out!'

Had a lovely voice, I did, before the T.N.T. got to me – 'Give us a song, Lil,' the other girls'd beg, soon as we come on the floor. It weren't easy to be heard over the din of the machines but I gave it me best: had 'em all off by heart after a month or two. *Pack up your Troubles, Home Fires, Tipperary, Sister Susie* ... and every girl's favourite when we was on the early shift, *Oh! How I Hate To Get Up In The Morning*.

'Oh yes!' says Margery, '*Splendid!*' like she's watching a flipping tennis match, 'You're doing *so* well, dear – nearly there!'

Nearly there! Not far to go! – that's what we'd tell each other, late afternoon when we was trying to make our quota – make sixty shells and you'd get a five shilling bonus, and that was five shillings we knew how to spend, all right. It was hard, boring work, filling shells – you had to pass the time somehow, so we told jokes and gossiped and sang. But soon enough I got the T.N.T. Tickle – that rasping cough that squatted on your chest and didn't go away – and the other girls started asking Maisie Briggs, so new to the work her skin was still pink, to sing instead.

'How long now?' I gasp, tears spilling out of my eyes. I ain't never been so tired, not after a twelve-hour Friday shift, not after the first night Danny come home on leave and we went out dancing all night, then came home and made love and talked and talked till it was morning.

'Not long, dear, not long, just breathe, just rest now,' – but for the first time, she don't sound too sure. I turn my head, searching for her face; see if I can read the truth in it. On the counterpane, my bright yellow hand's still grasping her white one like I'm hanging off a cliff and she's me rope. She ain't even wincing: used to it, I suppose.

'It's all right, is it? The baby?' The words are out before I can stop 'em. No time for anything between contractions but honesty. Hope she answers fast or I won't hear her over me own mooing. Her well-shaped eyebrows draw together, but she don't look worried – not quite. Not yet.

'Of course!' she says briskly. 'We'll have Baby out in a jiffy. Just a few more good pushes. Do you think you have it in you?'

I'm bloody sure I've got it in me, I think, like the old music-hall joke Danny used to tell, *and now I want it out of me!*

He was a scandal, was Danny. The other girls couldn't believe it when we started courting – me so quiet, apart from the singing that was, and him so bold. Truth is, he was the only man I ever met who could get me out me shell – he made a joke about that, too, you can be sure – oh Lord, how we laughed! First night we met, and all the times after, and it weren't just the beer – he knew how to have a good time all right. It was the same at the Front: he was the joker in the pack, keeping up the other men's spirits. I lost count of all the blokes from his company who sought me out when they demobbed, come to give condolences and say Danny always cheered 'em up, they couldn't've got through it without Danny. Some folks looked at us like we was from another planet, bright yellow all over with the T.N.T. in our skin and hair, but Danny never minded, though he could've had anyone.

'Look at me,' he'd say, 'stepping out with a Canary Girl! Better make sure I *tweet* you right!'

'Oh Danny!' I'd say, and thump him, but he'd always turn it into a cuddle, the cheeky blighter.

'Good… good… breathe, and keep going, keep going!' She's getting excited now – I can't hardly see, black creeping in round me vision.

'Oh Danny…' I groan.

A month before it all ended. Just a month. Just a week before he was due to go on leave. Not even a battle or a bullet – a fragment of shell, made no doubt by a German Mädchen in the Kaiser's factories. Right through the heart they said. Didn't know what'd got 'im.

He was so happy when I told him I was in the family way.

'That was quick work girl!' he said. 'They'll be gossiping about us down the canteen!' I didn't tell anyone till I was showing, of course, specially not the Misses. Some girls left when they was far enough gone, they was afraid what the work'd do to the baby, but I had to keep going. For the money. And for Danny. He was always so proud I was doing me bit. Even when my hair went ginger with the chemicals, he only told me he'd always fancied redheads.

'Could be worse,' I said. 'Some girls it goes green.'

Here comes a big one. It's like a storm cracking overhead; you can feel it coming then it's on you and you're deaf and blind and can't think of anything but *push push push*.

'Oh!' Marge clutches my hand harder. 'I can see the head! Marvellous! Keep it up, there's a good girl! Come on Lilian! You can do it!'

I can do it. I can do it, for Danny, for Danny and me, but I'm scared. I've felt the baby at night, moving around, thumping to be let out, feels like, and every time a little hard knobble pokes me belly from the inside I've wondered – is it a hand? Is it a foot? Is it… all there?

'Breathe … breathe … it's coming, it's coming, it's coming… PUSH!' cries Marge, and I breathe, and I breathe, and I sob, and I squeeze, and I cross my twisted fingers around hers –

Because you never know do you? What this stuff can do. It ain't barley-sugar we're packing in them shells: it's poison, right enough, even if it's slow and it don't affect everybody. Some girls get the cough, some get the headaches – all of us get the yellow skin, so yellow we got to eat separate from everyone else cos chairs, tables, plates, cups, whatever we touch turns yellow. Some girls' bosoms even got bigger after working in the factory a few months – they wasn't complaining, nor their husbands, but it makes you think: what else is it doing to you, to your insides? To anything inside you?

'PUSH!' yells Marge, right in my ear'ole. Next time they need a sergeant-major … 'PUSH, LIL!'

I'm mooing again, mooing and crying and pushing and gritting my teeth till the metal fills my mouth, just like back at the factory, that TNT taste you never could get rid of.

Used to be an orphanage on our street, and some of the poor mites was born wrong, you could tell; blind, or crippled, not enough fingers, or heads too small; smooth stumps where legs ought to be. God knows I'd love it all the same, but thinking of those babes has been enough to make me weep, these last weeks.

'There it is! The head's out!' she pants – and everything's loud and whirling and then the shoulders, and the rest of it in a rush, like riding the dizziest merry-go-round there ever was.

'A little boy!' she cries, 'Oh goodness, well done Lil, well done…'

But there's something in her voice. Like when folk talk to you at a funeral. There's something she ain't saying, and I can't see him, my baby, I can't see what's wrong. All those times I wished Danny could at least have seen his child – I never thought it might be a blessing if he never did.

'Give him to me,' I gasp. 'I want to see him. Please.'

She's wiping something with a towel, such a small little bundle it is; there's white waxy stuff and blood, lots of it. Mine or his?

'All right, Mrs Phillips,' she says, and I dunno why we're back on last name terms now, 'but you mustn't be… surprised, it's perfectly… I mean, I've never seen –'

Why ain't he crying?

'Give him to me,' I croak. 'I want to see.'

And suddenly, a warm squirming thing on my chest; under my clutching fingers a soft head with a little wet mop of black hair, just like his dad's. I feel along his squashy limbs, all curled up; ten fingers, ten toes. I touch his face, crumpled like a rosebud: two eyes, a nose, a mouth that's all gum. It's all there. It's all right. But why ain't he crying?

I raise my head to get a proper look – the effort nearly bloody kills me – and now I see what the midwife means. My little boy:

strong and healthy, four limbs present and correct, all his bits and bobs in place.

And bright daffodil yellow.

'They say it fades in a few months…' Marge is saying doubtfully. 'Otherwise, he's quite sound you know…'

'He's perfect,' I say, kissing his puffy lemon-coloured cheek with my buttercup lips. I can't help it: I'm crying with exhaustion and laughing so hard it's like Danny's back in the room. What a turn up!

'A canary boy! How your dad would've chuckled,' I murmur into his ear.

And he must understand, 'cos at last he opens his wide wet gummy yellow mouth, and he starts to sing.

Poems

Peaceful
Anwar Jaber

The Peace's Water

Life sits on her high chair and looks at me with a hidden smile. She knows that war had stolen our rainbow, and had left me as bare as a rock. Yes, I am a grey man, know nothing about the vivid perfumes, and my dreams are faded as old wood. Do you see these fissures on our earth? They are our girls' hearts; they need some water. Everything will be velvety when our thirsty souls find the water of peace.

The Peaceful Dresses

My mantle was red; I am the son of the wars, and all that you can see is my crippled remnants. I don't remember anything about the peaceful dresses, because our town brides were killed before their weddings, and our land's face was smashed by the unknown. Now, we are loveless and know nothing about the moon's tales. We are always looking for our lost dresses in this white and wide world. Here, we can't see our hands because they disappear in the mouth of war, and we can't hear our voices because they drown in its absent ocean.

The Peaceful Tent

We have a coloured tent that resembles the face of my mother, who spent her life in bringing peace from the remote wells to irrigate our dry souls. You know, I am a man from the east; my colour is different from that of my western friend, but in spite of this we are in deep intimacy which the moon lovers can't imagine. Yes, our tongues are different, but our souls are all descended from that peaceful tent.

Clearing
Nicholas McGaughey

Now I clear the forgotten field
of bramble-coil,
buttercup and foxglove
flaunting their colours
like bugles to the sky;
to find:
neat trenches,
strawberry faces, white without sun,
the guts of old potatoes
weeping in the spaded soil,
and rows of flat white markers
with names now faded,
of what was once hoped for,
and lost.

Another Rising
Anne Elizabeth Bevan

They shook the clay, damp and dank, from their shoulders,
their coats in rags, their spirits rested.
Germany calling, the rumble rose from the martyr's tombs;
a gentle tremor shivered the turf beneath.
Soldiers of old, of freedom, of courage,
marched the streets, their battle
past, or yet to come. They walked
amongst the rainbow warriors, the bee keepers,
the champions of light. Battle cries, colourful
on blank walls. Equality and freedom,
save the forests, the animals, gay rights.
Faced with a new war, not armed, no remit,
they dragged their riddled bodies back to the grave,
to rest until the love had passed,
their time not yet.

Left at the Cenotaph
Ness Owen

Left at the cenotaph
heard it all my life
a direction to the
centre of our small
town on the edge of
an island touching
the sea, it's there
opposite where you
catch the bus but never
stop to count Williams,
Owens, Pritchards
and Jones after Jones.
It was to be simple,
dignified to take away
the bareness left behind;
unassuming, except
when poppies are out.
Cornish granite crafted
by a German sculptor who
had to change his name.
The sailor frozen in bronze
looks landwards, the soldier
towards Tŵr, the mountain
of his youth but life continues
even in stone, moss and lichen
take hold, rock returning to
sand as they etch another name.

Armistice, 1918, San Francisco
James Toupin

Come what might,
they would assemble
to celebrate.

Late fashions of death,
of mustard gas and Browning gun,
could now be shut away

like gowns never to be worn again.
If they were afraid of armies
their fellows' breath might carry,

they could make the streets
their hospital, cheering peace
behind white masks.

Hope's false hygiene:
this foe would rush
the surgeon's no man's land.

Its world's war
observed no armistice.
Somewhere in the newsreels

my grandmother parades,
released for this
from care of her three children.

However present she was
in the anxiety
that raised me,

I will never find her face.
Her daughter recalled
brushing her hair.

Girl Looking Out
Sarah Deckro

Photo Exhibit
Lodz Ghetto, Poland

This is not what mother dreamed.
What father dreamed –
Grandmother dreamed,
As my hand curled their finger.

My hand,
Your hand,
Our hands pierce boundaries,
But cannot reach.
These hopes
Have already come to rest.

When the train stops,
When the tracks end,
What then?

Bone and ash,
Bones of my brethren
Weighing me down.
No stone remembers my name.

I want to say that
Life is more than ugliness.
I want to tell you…
But time is gone.

When you leave
I fear
I will disappear.
I wish you could save me.
But all you do is stand
And stare.

there are poppies and many other flowers
Rob Walton

let's have a dozen red roses growing
on remembered tables and forgotten deck chairs
to remind us of love

show me passion flowers and anemones sprouting
in school playgrounds where children link arms
and sing songs of peace

I want hydrangeas and hyacinths blooming
in the books and shelves and computers in libraries
smelling of tomorrows and not yesterdays

give me daisies and aquilegias flowering
on the counters of shops and bars and cafes
where people raise toasts to all of us

we want tulips and poppies spreading
to all continents and seas and skies
scented with hope

feast your eyes on rosemary and mint springing up
at family barbecues and picnics for friends
in all seasons

have a look at roses and sunflowers flourishing
in sheds and garages and outbuildings
where all is constructive

the people hope for daffodils and orchids blossoming
in sports halls and walking trails
where meetings and greetings are generous

I long to see dahlias and lilies carpeting
beaches and corridors and roofs
in a world where flowers are in charge

Coffee Table Diplomacy
Rob Walton

come back here to the conference table
come back for talk and coffee and cake
come and have Kaffee und Kuchen

come back here for a chin wag round our house
come back for talk and coffee and cake
come and have une tasse de café et un morceau de gâteau

come back here for jaw-jaw with fingers off triggers
come back for talk and coffee and cake
come and have pumpkin pie and an espresso

come back here to take the floor
come to talk, to dance, to eat and drink
come back here and get it bloody sorted

Living in the Country During the War
Ellery Akers

Every night now, I lie on cool sheets
and think of the burning. The sound of feet running
on gravel, the sound of fire louder than water.
I try not to look at the headlines
as I move from room to room in clean clothes
drinking a glass of ice water.
It's quiet here, but I feel uneasy.
Under the silence: the fire.
I drop a letter in a mailbox,
the lid closes
and under the clank
is the sound of the fire: the blur of the fire.
Women running on gravel in sandals.
I'm uneasy taking a bath. Gardening.
Walking under the deep shade of Douglas fir.
It's there under everything: the sound of the fire.
Women in sandals, running.

Poppy Day
Karen Ankers

war discarded
is not peace
but a hundred years of scar tissue
a thickened itching unhealed wound
that bleeds while we dig through
scabscaled memories

every year
in a silent minute
children are taught to celebrate blood
tiny redpinned chests
betray the death of innocence
and suddenly
a poppy is no longer
a summerflame flicker

petals fall
beneath the weight of hatechoked words
and pride that hides as love

Craiglockhart
Steven Jackson

'Many of us who came to the Hydro slightly ill are now getting
  dangerously well.'

This relief is as shocking as the bombs.

The day does not start by alarm.
I rise from a bed of white sheets.
The water I wash with is clean.
I dress, deliberate and slow.

These boots feel strange, in want of puttees.
The rucksack on my back is lighter now:
a book on birds, packed in place of ammo.
My head is free, having shelled the Brodie,
left it some other place, back in a dream –
a charnel house for the cast halves of tin skulls.

I start walking. The first steps
of my own 'ergotherapy'.
The hospital's doors are opened.
Wind greets me with a Scottish kiss.

But it does not hurt. Its force is affection,
if anything; the rough touch of a friend,
the hard hand of the father, whose calluses
brush the child's face to move its hair away.

Resurrection: the Sandham Memorial Chapel, Burghclere

Mantz Yorke

After Stanley Spencer's murals depicting his experience of World War I

Released from graves, they dump redundant crosses
before the seated Christ. To their left, comrades
glance up from trenches towards this resurrection,
perhaps for the first time believing death is no more
than a rest on the winding ascent to heaven.

Elsewhere, a convoy bears wounded into hospital;
obsessively, a shell-shocked soldier scrubs the floor
and others, under mosquito nets, are being told
the war that was supposed to end all wars
is over, and they can anticipate returning home.

You might imagine resurrection would pass down
a legacy of experience and understanding,
and that emergent souls would have encouraged us
to defy those who've assumed control and demand
we beat our ploughshares into swords.

The risen would be dismayed that their brief lives
have not prevented further inscriptions on the scroll
of inhumanity – Guernica, London, Stalingrad, Dresden,
Hiroshima, Grozny, Srebrenica, Baghdad, Gaza, Aleppo,
along with terrorism and agencies' black ops.

There's no New Jerusalem waiting to descend.
Only when we've stopped the bullets, the shells,
the bombs, the gas, can we ourselves construct it
from the rubble scattered across those graveyards
where poppies alone retain the nerve to bloom.

Sympathy for the Oppressed
Corie Feiner

Edward's vision for a new
day was so clear he had believed

the world was ready
for ascension –

But the pistol shot fired in Sarajevo plunged
the world into the clouds of war –

and his parade to paradise
became a vile stampede.
German measles became
'victory measles' ,

sauerkraut became
'victory cabbage' ,
a man who claimed to be a patriot
dragged a German-American

from his bed, stripped him
of his clothes, and publicly

whipped him until he kissed
the American flag.

Edward confessed.

He, too, was hyph-

enated. Part what he was – part
where he was –

his accent mis-
understood, his talk
of peace, vilified.
If you had struck him,
he would have turned
the other cheek,

if you had stolen his best white shirt,
he would have given you his cloak,

if you had told him
to spread hate,

he would have warned you
of the dangers within,

and told you the story
of how he bit his fingernails

to shreds when the soldiers knocked
on his door and told him of the battle
in which his father died.

He professed – *I have nothing*
but loathing for this foul
and unthinkable war.
At night, his house was splashed
with yellow paint –

At dawn, his neighbours crossed the street
to avoid his gaze –

How to make peace
when there was no peace?

How to explain that all of us
are, or once were, hyphenated?

How to explain that to be a patriot
is not to wipe an entire language
from this earth?
When asked if he would fight he said,
My country can take my last penny,
and my last drop of blood, but my soul,
my soul is my own.

My husband's great-uncle, Edward Steiner (1886-1956), was a prominent
WWI pacifist, speaker, writer, and professor at Grinnell College

The Grass is Waking in the Ground
Sarah Tait

How to describe it, that grass?
How to show its richness since it once broke free
under the bluest blue sky in that deep pause?
How to share this soft noon on these gentle slopes,
the rolling tumbling calm of summer
poured over hummocked hills
and around the trees and silent lines of stone
in all the tenderness of this bursting green?

To think how once it crept –
warmed each seeping sunrise to lushness
despite the chaos and the churning that came, and went,
with the sighs of a hundred years of humid afternoons
alive and awake in this fertiled ground
with just the slightest tremble
before the breeze rises and sweeps
as the last notes of the last post die.

The Catwick Blacksmith (*John Hugill*)
Elinor Brooks

Through two world wars he havens them in his forge
under the horseshoe nailed to the door

shines them up like buttons –
the halfpennies
the pennies –

hammers a coin to the post each time
a man goes off to fight

fixes it tight.

South Elnham St Michael
Middleton-on-the-Hill

Upper Slaughter
Stocklinch

Langton Herring
Herodsfoot

Pipe Aston
Flixborough

Herbrandston
Woolley

High Toynton
Catwick

Nether Kellett
Arkholme

All come safely back
to villages made thankful twice

where poppies grow in innocent fields
where families rejoice.

Music in the Battlefield
Martin Willitts, Jr

In the lull between the shooting,
I played my flute so quietly
music notes were blackberries.

For a moment, the fields were silent, my song
drifting across barbed wire, broken wheels, dying
split open horses, to the men agonising,
cauterised their wounds.

The quiet finds what needs to be lifted up,
and lifts it.

War Diary in 1/72 Scale
Peter Kenny

Ate the carrots, like he said.
I crouch below the botched assembly
of British bombers: Hampden,
Halifax, Lancaster, Short Stirling,
strung from the Artex ceiling
crews glued in cockpits, curled in turrets
behind their Browning 303s.

I want them to fly the sortie
I built them for, some Merlin magic
to spark their plastic into life,
to cross the moonless landing, to pound
his unsuspecting country
where the TV occupies the night
and he takes shelter in cider.

Headlights from the street outside
shaft through a parting in the curtains,
add fleeting shadow squadrons
to the ceiling. Dad scrambles in the hall,
twists the handle of my door.
Like the turret gunners, I'm wide-eyed,
expecting all his Messerschmitts.

Almost Standing Still
Peter Shaver

There's a blurred photograph
of my great-grandfather
grinning
in a uniform in the snow,
with, I think,
his father Emery
and sister Pearl.

They're both standing
slightly apart
from him and
everyone's wearing coats.
His sister looks
happy, surprised to see him,
or to see him like that.
The father's smiling, too.
But his eyes are shadowed
by his hat.

The trees are black, bare,
and the mountains rolling low
behind them,
all pushed in and back,
caging around
their bodies.

Everything looks tilted.
Like the whole world's
moving forward.
They're the only three things
almost standing still.

Obscured behind his back,
a dark car
lies waiting.
I can't tell
if he's getting ready
to go
or just come home.

Burdock
Gerald McCarthy

Remember when summer
    clung to you like cotton,
    like the barbed wire fence
you pulled up,
    crossing into an open meadow
the creek misted over
    from the morning's rain –
and it felt as if
you could run all day,
    past the sheds
down through pine woods.

Memory, the doctor says –
    is not a mirror,
you look away
    from what you think
you saw and
    rediscover
something else.
Like some fingers
    pulling at your sleeve,
a kind of blue –
    you keep seeing
just out of reach.

I will tell you how it was
Nina Murray

I will tell you how it was: one morning
all the old people came out. Rain
washed them down the frames of their windows
where they had sat so long, their own etched portraits.
They polished their buttons, those old people did,
their belt buckles, too, and the lost armies' insignia,
the locks on their cracked portupees. Their purses.
They pulled out hats with startled veils and the thread-thin
gloves they'd been saving for when they'd be put into coffins,
and they shook out the naphthalene pills gnawed thin.
They kept coming out. They carried their ancient selves
across streets, until they stood in the old city centre,
in front of the best hotel, quietly singing.

The Return
Peter De Ville

After Tu Fu 713-770 A.D.

Cliffs of scarlet cloud glow in the west,
The blob of sun dissolves in the earth.

Suddenly, the sparrows stop chittering at the gate.
The stranger steps into his house from thousands of miles.

My wife is astonished that I still exist.
She is bewildered, but smears away her tears.

I was drifting dust in the blast of the world's rage.
It can only be fate that has carried me alive.

The fence gate is filled with neighbours' faces
Sighing and gulping, with flowing, easy tears.

My leg just holds, my arm is just a ghost,
And I'm afraid my head is torn and soft.

In the deep night we light a new candle
And see each other's face, finally, like a dream.

The Wheat
Peter De Ville

Chevrons upside down, you're still the general.
It's the jaunty, single, ticked-off leaf,
saluting grey-green army, knobble-kneed.
Not one is cowed. Straight to the sun.
No wispy, fainting barley, poppy prance.

Steeled to attention

tick-tight ranks.

That green grub of a wood
has been extinguished.

Per ardua ad astra.

You sweep to the sky.

The field is yours.

Light
Valerie Bence

As we spilled out onto the street, laughing
on this sad, memorial day
I saw the shaft of light
without knowing what it was.
Look I said *the moon is shining*
through a hole in the clouds.
We all looked up, heads tipped back.
Hemmed-in by city streets and rooftops
it pierced the dark, like the blitz searchlights of a forties film
seeking prey – but it was motionless, almost solid –
was it beaming up or beaming down?

the moon had never been that bright.
The mood changed, there was a frisson of – something,
obviously it was not the moon
but what could tear a hole in the night sky;
a film shoot, special effects, an alien sphere?
It felt like magic.

On the news the next day,
an installation for the Great War,
a giant pillar of white light
unannounced – *Artangel spectra* –
such a piercing straight line
sucking up all those lost boys
each held newborn in their mother's arms
as I had held mine;
given names for so short a time
until carved in wood or stone
or light.

I looked then at my children
all older now than so many taken
and the beam became the scream
of all the silent women.

Written on 4th August 2014 London, on seeing *Artangel spectra* by Japanese artist Ryoji Ikeda, after my daughter's birthday meal, on the centenary of the outbreak of WWI

(https://www.artangel.org.uk/project/spectra/)

For Jean Jaurès
Norman Francke

You knew wars do not start
when the first shot is fired,
but twenty years earlier
when the diplomats
get wasted at press balls;
when students are discouraged
from studying languages;
and priests spend more time looking
after angel's faces on war memorials
than starving children.

A few days before the announcement
of a state of 'imminent risk of war'
and the first of the four-limb amputees,
you, and your friends said

'Ce n'est pas encore la guerre!'
'Dies ist noch nicht der Krieg!'
'It is not yet war!'

There will be time
to organise a general strike
of all European workers; there is still time
to plant apple trees in Flanders.

On the same day that Zaharoff,
who sold his machine guns
to both sides,
and donated the monkey house to
the Paris Zoo,
became commander of the Legion
d'honneur;

over dinner, at the Café du Croissant
in the rue Montmartre
they shot you from behind
(your killer was acquitted,
your wife ordered
to pay the court fees).

Under the chestnut trees' chandeliers
there is a dance floor, like in Renoir's paintings.
This, too, is Europe; and deep beneath, in the coal seams
those already condemned to death, sing
to their jackhammers
of love.

Retracing his Steps to the Gunpowder Store
Jane Aldous

Fancy this place still being here,
the old stone warehouse beside the harbour.
We never stopped.
Four years of loading and unloading munitions,
artillery, gunpowder, engine parts, ropes,
chains, fuels and tools.

Who knew then how many warships
there'd be on the Forth
and how many uniformed men.
All the bodies that were stored here too,
in the midst of all that clamour of planes,
lorries, trains, landings and disembarkations.

All those years since I was last here.
Can't believe it's all intact but shuttered up
with no purpose, surrounded by high flats,
concrete houses and tied-up yachts.
The rail tracks are going nowhere and there's
a blue teapot cast in the debris of Middle Pier.

Now a listed building in poor repair, the Gunpowder Store was built in 1842 on
Middle Pier, Granton Harbour, Edinburgh and was put into service during WWI
and WWII

Footnote to Tet
Ken Farrell

Before today on the pool deck
I'd have sworn I'd never seen the lunette
scar umbrella'd two inches above Mom's
left nipple; she lazed in the chaise longue and said
when young I'd run fingers along it and hum
a non-song while she waltzed me to sleep.
A Viet Cong Captain, face charred
by napalm, was Mom's patient in Vinh Long.
He snatched a pen from her hand
leaned forward, punched into her chest
and was shot dead and dropped from gurney to deck;
Mom fell back and their bloods pooled.
She sat among crimsoned gauze and donned
latex gloves to self-stitch the wound.
Just then sirens rang:
mortar shells rained,
the moon falling, bursting, shaking
earth, air, tent, as she slippery-pinched the gash.
That's why the scar, she said. She sat beside the dead
Captain, thought long of me, though I was years away,
and tremblingly needled her gory breast.

Talk of War
Nick Westerman

There is talk of war
Up and down the borders
Talk in the East
Talk in the West

There is talk of war
In the guttural tones of Polish and Russian
The twang of America
And the softness of Chinese whispers

There is talk of war
Of settling old scores
Reheating cold wars
Avenging festering sores

There is talk of war
Each time
We lack the courage
To talk of peace

ABOUT THE AUTHORS

With so many authors involved, including biographical notes here would tip the book into another section of sixteen pages. You can find details of *all* our authors and poets on our website: www.arachnepress.com.

ABOUT ARACHNE PRESS

Arachne Press is a micro-publisher of (award-winning!) short story and poetry anthologies and collections, novels, including a Carnegie Medal nominated young adult novel, and a photographic portrait collection.

We are expanding our range all the time, but the short form is our first love. We keep fiction and poetry live, through readings, the Solstice Shorts Festival, workshops, exhibitions and all things to do with writing.

Follow us on Twitter:
@ArachnePress
@SolShorts

Like us on Facebook:
ArachnePress
SolsticeShorts2014

Events

Arachne Press is enthusiastic about live literature and we make an effort to present our books through readings.

The Solstice Shorts Festival

(http://arachnepress.com/solstice-shorts)

Now approaching its fifth year, Solstice Shorts is all about time: held on the shortest day of the year on the Prime meridian, stories, poetry and song celebrate the turning of the moon, the changing of the seasons, the motions of the spheres, and clockwork!

We are always on the lookout for other places to show off, so if you run a bookshop, a literature festival or any other kind of literature venue, get in touch; we'd love to talk to you.

Workshops

We offer writing workshops suitable for writers' groups, literature festivals and evening classes, which are sometimes supported by live music – if you are interested, please get in touch.